The M

Revised 2020 Edition

Sal Nudo

Printed in the United States of America.

Cover photo by KoolShooters from Pexels
Editing assistance in 2014 version from Mariam Pera and Esther Reisberg

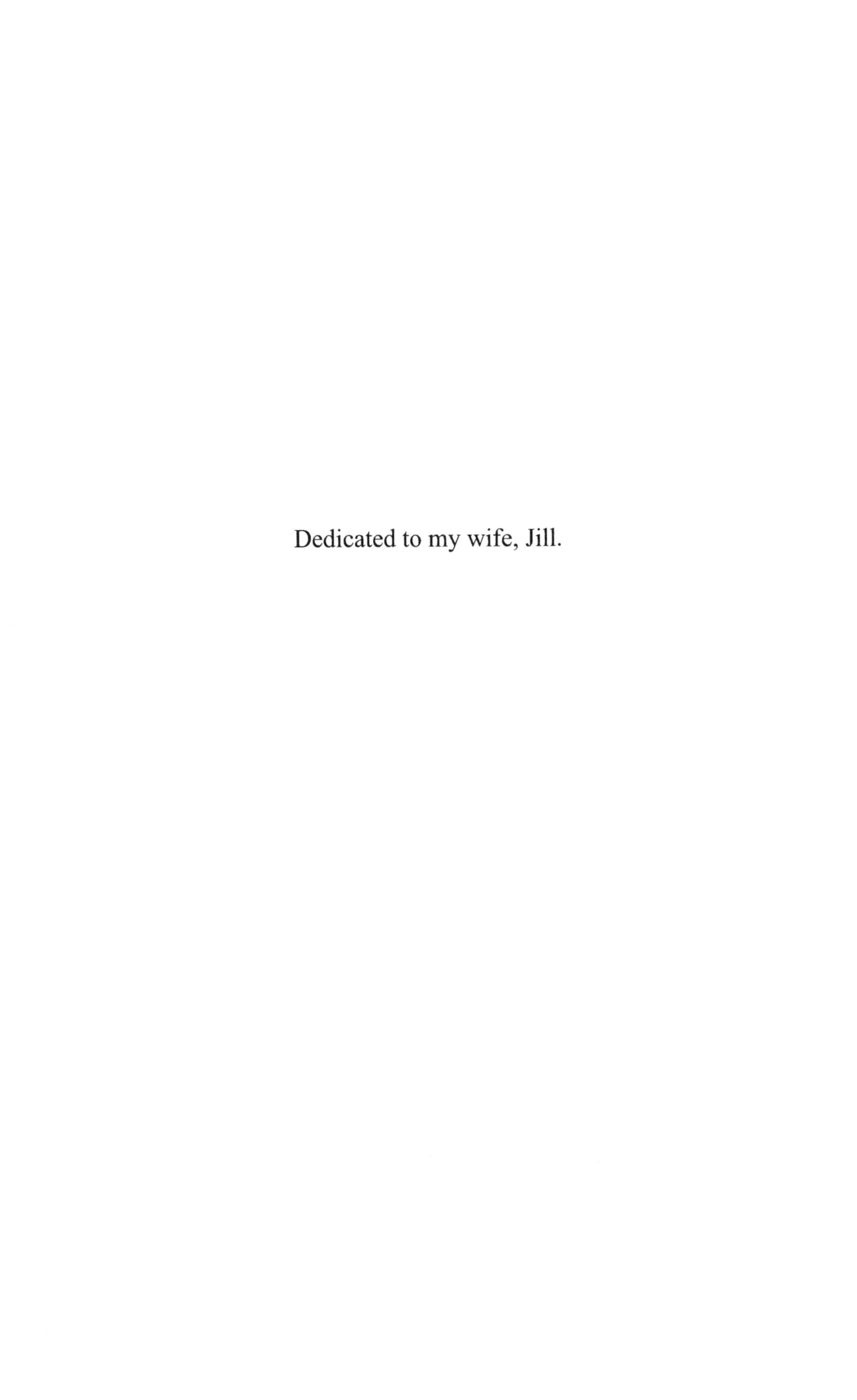

Dedicated to my wife, Jill.

Other Books by Sal Nudo

Phantom Reunions
The Newspaperman
Far From Mars: Nine Creative Nonfiction Stories Featuring People and Places in Champaign-Urbana

"The man who has won millions at the cost of his conscience is a failure."

- B.C. Forbes

Chapter 1

Early December 2004

I wolfed down the second of my two Taco Bell bean burritos, no onions, just as the public transit bus pulled to a squeaky halt next to the bus stop.

Through the half-tinted windows, I could see Trevor's thin, hunched shape heading toward the side exit. He saw my car right away and walked toward it in that sort of hop-walk way he had, eyeing me as he chatted up Chad, his skinny boyfriend.

Trevor, my twenty-five-year-old brother who was five years younger than me, opened the front passenger door of my car, letting in an acrid smell of bus fumes. One of the drawstrings poking out of his hood on his ratty-looking sweatshirt was shorter than the other, all gnarled and cut up. "Hey, bro," he said, leaning into my car. He held out his hand for me to shake. I grabbed it and shook quickly.

"Can we give Chad a lift to Mahomet? He needs to get something from his dad's place."

"Mahomet? That's a little out of the way."

"Come on, man. I'll give you gas money."

"Yeah, right. When?"

“Right now.” Trevor pulled out a five-dollar bill and flipped it to me.

I handed it back to him. “Keep your money, Trevor.” I glanced at Chad, who was waiting a few feet behind Trevor. He was looking scruffy with a noticeable five o’clock shadow and his dark curly hair uncombed. What did these guys do all day?

I peered out at the desolate shopping mall plaza and the massive, pothole-filled parking lot sprawled out in front of it, hardly a car anywhere. Country Lane Shopping Center, a bustling strip mall when I was a kid, had gone bust during the last decade.

“I know it’s a big favor, Alex,” Trevor said in a softer voice, “but I’ll owe you one. You know neither of us has a car. Do us this solid.”

Trevor didn’t have to remind me that he was carless. Two years ago he’d smashed his Ford Mercury Tracer into a tree, wasted and laughing like a madman after it had happened. He was slapped with a DUI, and in the intervening time period had refused to try and get his license back. My parents and I could not discern any particular reason why.

“All right, get in,” I said with a coldness that matched the frigid air streaming into my car. "Hurry up, it's fricking freezing."

Trevor nodded at Chad, who slipped into the backseat. Trevor climbed in front, and right away I could smell pot in the fibers of his clothes.

Just then it started snowing. "Wonderful," I said, peering out the windshield.

Chad thanked me for the ride and then started tapping the back of my headrest as if he were playing the drums. I looked at him in the rearview mirror. "Could you please not do that?"

"Sorry," Chad replied. And then, in a deep, businesslike voice, he said, "Talk radio: the choice of serious-minded citizens everywhere."

Trevor stifled a laugh, which pissed me off. "What have you guys got against talk radio? Sorry it's not the Grateful Dead or whatever it is you guys listen to."

They both thought this statement was hilarious and burst out laughing. I changed the radio to a classic rock station, well-known songs that were agreeable to all. Chad was singing along to an Eagles song in a surprisingly good falsetto.

"We appreciate the ride," Trevor said, turning to look at me.

I nodded. It wasn't uncommon for Trevor to call me and ask to be picked up from somewhere after I got off work. I usually obliged without asking too many questions, no matter where in town I picked him up or took him. But today was different: I hadn't expected to see Chad and wasn't aware of the drive to Mahomet, a small town fifteen minutes away from Champaign.

"Where am I taking you guys after Mahomet?" I asked.

"My place," Chad said. "If you don't mind."

Minutes later, at the corner of Duncan and Bradley, Trevor said, in a pensive voice, "There's your old condo."

I glanced to my right and looked at it, the first residence I'd ever owned. I'd lived there by myself for four years, prior to marrying my wife, Emily. We live in a charming house in an older section of central Champaign, and it was difficult not to regard the time at my condo as a lonelier period of my life. I didn't miss the interchanging neighbors who surrounded me, nor the late-night fights between the revolving-door couples above and across from me. The boisterous parties that sometimes took place, the barking dogs, crying babies, the sound of other people having sex as I tried to sleep—all of it was long in my past.

I took a left on Duncan onto Bradley and drove about a half mile to Staley Road, where I took a right and headed toward U.S. 150, a convenient backroad surrounded by vast Illinois cornfields. From there, we'd catch Interstate 74.

An oddly placed cemetery was located at the intersection of 150 and Staley, and that's where I took a left. Once we hit the interstate, it was an approximately fifteen-minute drive to Mahomet.

Chad was flicking his cigarette lighter on and off as he hummed a song. Then, above the din of another song on the radio, he sang out "Heroine is so passeeeee!"

Slushy snow was pelting my windshield. I turned to look at Trevor, who was stifling a laugh. Curly locks of his hair edged out of his hood, and I could make out his half-closed stoner eyes as he stared at the road zipping by, underneath the headlights of my Ford Focus. "Aw, rabbits!" he yelled, confusing me.

Chad squealed with laughter and clapped his hands. Then he sang a lyric I recognized: "I want to ride my bicycle, I want to ride my bi—*cyc*!"

Trevor exploded with laughter and then said "Tango and Cash" in an enunciated, prim manner. This in turn excited Chad, who tried out another song lyric.

"You guys are weird," I said, turning up the radio even louder.

Except for the blaring music in the car—I'd changed the radio to an alternative rock station at Chad's request—the rest of the ride was quiet. Chad was in and out of his dad's place in no time and eased back into the car saying nothing, looking subdued.

"Are you best friends with your pops now?" Trevor asked, turning to look at Chad.

"Pshh. That would be a negative, boyfriend."

Back on U.S. 150, a plain stretch of road from which one could visit the mighty metropolis of Foosland, population one hundred twenty-three, numerous thoughts ricocheted around my head like wayward ping pong balls. I thought of work and household tasks and my wife and the baby we were trying to have with a desperation that was making me frazzled. I stared at the pavement ripping by, my brain a vacuum, sucking up thoughts and roiling them around, ruminating, worrying, relaxing, and forgetting.

I was jarred back to reality from this state of absent-minded duality—a sort of airy nothingness mixed with consequential events—when the power in my car died. It happened just as I turned right onto Staley Road from U.S. 150. The steering wheel locked up and I could feel the power go out of the car, which kept rolling for several seconds after the engine died. Just before it stopped I managed to pull over to the side of the road and could hear the sound of crunching gravel, and then no sound at all—it was an unexpected and spooky moment.

"Shit," I said.

"What happened? Try to start it back up," Chad ordered, leaning his head in between the two front seats.

His bossy tone was irritating, but I did what he said. There wasn't a peep from the car when I turned the key, nor did it help when I pressed the accelerator to try to get some juice. I turned the key several more times, all wasted efforts.

"Shit," I said again.

We got out of the car, popped the hood, and peered inside, two gay guys and me, someone who knew nothing about cars and made his living behind a computer as a copywriter of hobby products.

“Looks fine to me,” said Chad, as if he were a licensed mechanic. I couldn’t find anything under the hood that looked out of whack either.

“No, it’s a belt,” Trevor said. “Look.” With black fingernail polish adorning the fingernail on his index finger, he pointed at a specific area of the engine that Chad and I hadn’t noticed.

We all three leaned in closer to the heated engine, which was comforting to be next to in the cold air. Sure enough, right in the center of the car’s innards, just to the left of the engine, was a black rubber belt that had ripped apart, its two formerly attached ends now frayed and jutting outward like a once-blessed union gone awry.

Staring at the torn belt, I breathed in the frigid air and noticed it had stopped snowing. That was something in our favor. “Well, I can call Emily. Wait, I think she’s at her book club. Damn.”

“We’ll have to get a tow truck,” Trevor said.

I turned to him. “Do you have your cell phone?”

“No. Service got cut off temporarily.”

I turned to Chad. “What about you?”

“Unlike my debit and credit cards,” Chad replied in a dainty voice, “I *do* leave home without my cell phone. I was late on my bill this month and last, honey. She ain't even in service."

Both Trevor and Chad laughed at this.

"Geez, guys," I said. "You gotta be kidding me."

"What about *you*?" Trevor challenged. "Where's your cell phone?"

I was too mad to admit that it had been foolish not to bring my phone as well, but for me, it was par for the course. Emily had had to plead with me to purchase one in the first place, and now that she had won that battle, the next step was getting me to actually carry it around and use it. In a world suddenly gone crazy with phones, the trend had not yet connected with me.

"I don't have one either," I admitted. "Let's start walking toward Bradley. It's a hike, but I don't see what else we can do."

"It's fucking cold," Chad snapped. "I'm not walking to Bradley. There are houses just right over there," he said, pointing in the direction we'd just come from.

I couldn't remember how close the nearest house was, but there was something about knocking on doors for help that felt wrong to me. I didn't want to unnecessarily scare any families or lonely old women as they settled in for the evening. It felt weird and invasive.

"I don't know. What if we go that way and there aren't any houses?" I said to Chad. "Or what if the nearest house that way is no closer than the house on Staley Road and no one's home? We'll have walked all that way and we'll be *farther* from home, not closer. If you really want to find a house, I'm positive there's one on this road, about halfway between here and Bradley."

"What if we go to that *one* house," Chad responded, not missing a beat, "and no one's home there? I'd prefer to take my chances with the cluster of houses that are along here, much closer by," he said, sweeping his arm backward.

"You can't see anything down that way," I retorted. "It's too dark. Who knows if there are even houses along 150."

"But there *are* houses on this road," Chad insisted.

"Do you actually remember seeing them?"

Chad paused and then said, "Yes! I know there are."

"What do you think?" I asked Trevor.

"I want to get high, bro. Where's the goods?" he asked Chad.

Chad dug into his pocket, pulling out a hash pipe.

"What in the world?" I asked my brother, vexed. "We're in the middle of nowhere, my car is busted, it's freezing, and you want to get high?"

"This isn't the middle of nowhere, Alex," Trevor countered. "And Chad's right. I'm sure there are houses closer to where we are now than the one you want to head off to. We should head back that way."

"Have some," Chad said to me, thrusting his lighter and hash-filled pipe into my stomach. "It'll relax you before we start knocking on doors."

"I don't smoke that stuff."

"Well, you should right now," Chad said. He stepped closer to me in a menacing way, touching the lighter and pipe on my closed, freezing fists that had no gloves.

"Fucking quit it, you freak!" I lashed out, feeling outvoted and angry. "All right then. Let's head back that way. "But if you guys—"

"Is that man dead?" Trevor asked.

Caught off guard by my brother's cryptic question, Chad and I ceased glaring at each other and looked in front of my car, thinking a deceased man was sprawled out in front of it.

"No, over there!" Trevor shouted, correcting us.

Across the street, a moaning man was lying on his back, right in front of the cemetery. From our vantage point it was impossible to make out his features, but he looked to be in pain.

"Come on!" Trevor shouted, rushing off toward the fallen figure. Chad gaped at me, a strained look on his face. It appeared he didn't want to go over there any more than me, but Trevor's urgent tone had a jolting effect, making us forget about our current predicament. Suddenly concerned that the man was really hurt, I raced off after my brother with Chad in tow, my car and the hash pipe forgotten about.

Chapter 2

Trevor got there first, crouching down to the prone man's level and saying something to him that I couldn't hear, probably asking how bad he was hurt or what had happened.

"Give me a sec," the old man said, his voice croaky and tense. He was writhing on the gravel with his back arched and his left hand underneath it. Trevor stood up and stepped back, glancing at Chad and I.

"If you have a phone," I said to the old man, "we can call someone for you. The three of us don't have one—hard to believe, I know."

His back collapsed to the ground, and he let out a sigh that produced a gust of breath into the night air. "Hold on, I'll be okay. I've got some pills."

It was difficult watching the guy make his way back up. He placed both of his gloved hands on the ground and sat up in a ginger, careful way, wincing as he did so. None of us thought to help him, but he seemed like the type of guy who wouldn't have accepted our assistance anyway. Turning to his side, he pushed on his right hand

and struggled upward; first on two knees; then one knee; and one final surge until he was upright, his stance delicate and a bit unsure. The guy turned around and gave us a crooked smile. "It's hell getting old," he stated.

Trevor chuckled and looked at Chad, who was eyeing the stranger with a curious look. I was shuffling my feet, waiting for someone to say something.

"But I'm fine!" the man continued in a hearty manner, laughing it off. "My name's David Kendrick. I heard some commotion over there by your car—sounded like some arguing going on—and I came trotting over to see what was up. I slipped on this little ice patch and, well, I guess you all saw the results of *that*."

He appeared to be in his seventies. The rugged look on his face and his crinkly eyes belied what I could tell was a youthful, energetic spirit. He was wearing a dark stocking cap, and I could see white wisps of his hair poking out from underneath. His white goatee gave him a trendy, man-of-the-world look that inspired trust and confidence. To me, the good-natured charm he displayed in the midst of obvious physical pain was endearing. Though my feelings would change later, David Kendrick struck me at first as someone I was glad to know.

"So, is it car trouble?" David inquired, nodding toward my Ford.

"Yeah, it's a busted belt," I said. "You got a phone we can use?"

"I do!" he said with glee. "Happy to assist. Come back this way with me. My car's back here."

We followed David around the cemetery's circular gravel road, which crunched as we walked on it. David was limping along as the three of us hovered nearby, not wanting to pass him up.

"Are you visiting a grave?" Trevor asked.

"Yes," David said. "My son's grave. He passed away in his late twenties. Internal complications that were never quite clear to us."

"Oh, I'm so sorry," Trevor said.

David approached his car and turned, looking at Trevor. "Thank you, young man, that's kind. Jared was a wonderfully spirited kid. I visit his grave more and more these days."

David looked up at the sky. He removed his stocking cap and mussed his thick white hair with his hand. "I don't have much these days," he informed us. "I'm a wealthy man, yes. And I've accomplished and done a lot in life, but I feel like I no longer have much."

I looked at Trevor and Chad to gauge their reactions; to my surprise, both of them had looks of concern and sympathy on their faces.

"Do you have any other kids?" Chad asked.

"No. Phyllis and I just had Jared. It tore us up when he left this world, and I'm sad to say that it ruined our marriage in many ways. But I suppose I can't blame Jared's death on everything in that department."

His old-man regrets were getting tiresome. It was hard for me not to ask for his phone again. I jumped up and down a few times to indicate I was freezing my ass off.

"Oh, the phone!" David remembered.

He opened the car door and leaned into the front seat to retrieve it. As he did, I looked at Chad. He was whispering something to Trevor.

It took me a few minutes to arrange a tow truck. After telling the guy where we were stranded, I handed the phone back to David. "Thank you *so* much," I said. "Who knows what we would have done without you."

"Would have been knocking on doors," Chad said.

"You betcha," David said. "What are all of your names?"

We told him and he seemed to appraise us in a new light, as if we were suddenly more important to him.

"I've got a favor," he said out of nowhere, "and I'm willing to give you all fifty bucks each to help me out. Interested?"

He was looking at me, waiting for an answer, so I managed to muster out, "Sure, uh, maybe. What is it?"

"When you get back to wherever you're going, simply mail off a letter for me. I'll be heading back to Mahomet soon, and if you boys help me out with this task, it's one less thing I have to remember to do."

I looked at Trevor and Chad, thinking this guy wasn't playing with a full deck.

"It's a nice offer, sir," Chad said, "but fifty bucks each for mailing a letter for you ... that seems excessive. I don't get it."

I nodded, agreeing with Chad's assessment of this bizarre request. Trevor was staring at the old man with quizzical eyes; the sympathy he'd shown toward David just moments before had transformed to curiosity.

"Fellas," David said with a cockeyed smile, "I'm a wealthy, wealthy man, as I stated, and I'm no longer young, as I'm sure you can tell. I have nothing but time and money to waste. I don't desire to travel and don't have expensive tastes. Nor does my wife, who is incapacitated and who has barely spoken to me these past few decades anyway. My experience is that when someone offers you easy money, you *take it* and don't ask questions. I'm not asking you to do anything illegal here."

Trevor stepped forward. "Give me the letter then. I'll mail it."

David stared at my brother for a moment, looking pleased. "That's a good lad. One second."

Lad. What an old-fashioned word, I thought.

After burrowing into his car once again, David turned to hand Trevor the letter, which was in a common white envelope.

"Who's it addressed to?" I asked.

"A friend of mine in Florida. It's a perfectly legal, friendly letter. I really appreciate you guys doing this." He reached into his wallet and started shuffling bills in his hand. Good to his word, David handed each of us fifty dollars.

I felt like I was in some bizarre movie all of the sudden. Our night had taken a strange turn.

"And there's much more of that where it came from. Do me my favors, make some easy money."

We all three looked at one another.

"You mean," Chad said, "you'll pay us more money in the future to do other favors?"

"Correct. And more than just fifty dollars down the road."

"What kind of favors?" I asked. "And how do we get a hold of you?"

"Easy favors. And how about you get a hold of me right here in this beautiful old cemetery. We'll meet right here."

Beautiful old cemetery. I looked around at the ramshackle headstones and ragged-looking grounds. Who was he kidding?

On cue, a gust of wind came shrilling by. It felt like a warning to say no, to turn around, head back to my car, and leave this weirdo to his rich-man isolation.

"Count me in," Chad said. "I'm sick of being broke all the time. But I'm googling you later to see what you're all about."

David didn't seem to know or care what googling was.

"I'm down too," Trevor said.

David turned to me. "And you?" he asked, his head tilted like a curious dog trying to decipher his master's words.

I was put off by everything that had happened tonight: the trip to Mahomet with Chad and the stalled car; the freezing weather and snow; the company I was keeping, which included this eccentric loony who nearly put out his back and was now trying to lull us into some game. I also didn't appreciate how Chad and Trevor had volunteered their services without consulting me first. After all, *I* was the one with the car who could get them to the cemetery to meet David.

Given all this, I'm not sure why I was so agreeable, even half cordial, as I answered David. I had a good job that I liked and didn't need his cash as much as Trevor and Chad did. But there was something inviting about David's sales pitch. It intrigued me that he was a wealthy man with nowhere to go and no one to spend his money on. Despite some doubts, I suppose the thought of earning easy money for performing simple tasks was appealing.

"I've, I've got a wife," I stammered. "We want a baby." The

statement sounded panicky and sissified in the cold night air, but there it was. "Extra cash would be nice," I continued, trying to redeem myself. "I just won't do anything that gets us in trouble. Not with a wife and a kid in our future."

"Understood," David responded. "Let's let things proceed as they may." And with that vague directive he offered us a parting wave. "Meet me back here in two days, same time. I'll have another simple job. Well worth your while."

David turned and opened his car door, bending down like molasses to haul himself in. "Well worth your while," he repeated in quiet voice, almost to himself.

Chapter 3

"That ... was ... weird," Chad said, as we headed back to my car. The three of us were walking close together at a brisk clip, perhaps an unspoken effort to warm each other up. I was in the middle, looking down and watching the air flow from my mouth. Trevor was to my left, seemingly content with the way things had gone down, his money shuffling in his hands as he counted it. In the background, I could hear David's car crunching atop gravel, traveling in the opposite direction, leaving the cemetery. A sudden burst of wind further numbed my face and ears, which I covered with cold hands in an attempt to keep them protected. I hoped the tow truck wouldn't take long.

"It was weird," I agreed.

"Are we really going back in two days?" Chad asked.

"I am," Trevor said. "Let's see what his next little job is."

"I don't like it," I said, "so I probably won't be returning. If you guys want to come back here, you'll have to find your own way."

This seemed to take the wind out of their sails, and Chad reverted to the juvenile sing-song game they'd played together earlier in my car. "Desperado," he crooned in an aggressive voice, trying to get

Trevor to respond.

But Trevor wasn't biting. "Jesus, Alex. The guy offers us easy cash, and you want to bail. You told him yes. Why are you changing your mind?"

"Forget him," Chad said. "It's more cash for us if he bails. We can find a way out here ourselves."

"It's not that," Trevor snapped, forcing Chad and I to stop and look at him. "We're in this together, guys, like a team. Let's see how it plays out. Maybe the poor guy is just looking for friendship. Did you hear what he said about his wife? And man, his son died when he was just in his twenties—how sad is that?"

Trevor was being sincere, but David made me leery. I halfway regretted accepting his money, in fact. What if the stupid letter was part of some illegal scheme? I didn't want to get involved with something dangerous or unlawful.

"You can think about it," Chad told me. "Give it a day or two, and if you don't want to go on Thursday, we'll scrounge a ride, maybe take a cab."

The thought of these two skinny, money-hungry guys returning to the bleak cemetery in the cold forced me—against my better instincts—to want to be a part of the action. Maybe Trevor was right: we were sort of a team.

I peered down Staley Road looking for headlights, longing to be in the warm cab of the tow truck. "Okay then," I said. "We'll come back out here on Thursday, see what his other job is." Trevor and Chad looked at each other, smiled, and high-fived.

"But the minute this guy asks us to do something not on the level, I'm out, and so are you guys. I'm in as long as everything's above board."

"Above board," Chad quipped, making fun of my choice of words.

"Wipe your nose," I told him. "There's snot coming out of it."

"All *right*, guys!" Trevor yelled, slapping me on the back. "This is gonna be fun. Now, where's that hitter?"

We agreed that Trevor would mail the letter. They walked home from the towing place since it wasn't far from where they lived, and I called a cab.

I got home and turned up the furnace in our drafty two-story house to thaw my bones out, savoring the warmth. Emily walked in fifteen minutes later and we microwaved leftover macaroni and cheese.

"We met this guy at a cemetery where my car died, Em," I said. We were sitting on stools around the kitchen's middle counter, "food island" as I liked to call it. Emily looked up from the magazine she was reading, a curious look on her pretty face. Her blonde hair was pulled back in a ponytail, and her beautiful blue eyes sparkled under the recessed lighting of our kitchen.

"And?" she said, reaching for her ice water and taking a sip, looking cute and refined with her pinky pointing outward.

"Well, he was injured," I ventured, all at once thinking she'd disapprove of how I'd accepted David's fifty dollars.

"Oh. What happened? Is he okay?"

"Yeah, he's fine. He slipped on some ice and we helped him up. It wasn't a big deal."

"That's good," she replied, looking down again and flipping a page in her magazine.

"Yeah. He was a rich old guy. He offered us fifty bucks each to do a favor for him."

Emily looked up. "What was the favor?"

"He … well, we heard him fall down and ran over to him. This was right after my car stalled. So we got to talking to him, and he said he needed us to mail a letter of his. He said he'd pay us fifty bucks each to do it. Chad and Trevor kind of jumped at the chance, and I said I'd do it, too."

She frowned. "Weird he'd give all three of you all that money for mailing a letter."

"I know. We all thought the same thing. We told him that."

"But you took his money anyway?"

"Yeah, I did. *We* did."

"Alex," she said in a disapproving tone, her brow furrowed in disapproval. "Where is the letter going?"

"Florida."

"Hmmm," she mused.

"What?"

"Was it just a regular letter?"

"Yeah. He said it was going to a friend he has down there."

"Well, I don't get it."

I chuckled. “Yeah. And here’s the kicker: he wants us to meet him again so we can do him another favor.”

“I don’t like it, Alex. He sounds weird.”

“I was thinking it’d be a good way for Trevor to get some easy money.”

“So let him do it on his own.”

“How would he get to the cemetery? He needs *me* for a ride.”

“He’s got friends. He can manage.”

“Em, I’d like to see this through with him. He’s excited about it. You know how he is. I don’t want him to go down some wayward path with this David guy.”

“That’s the guy’s name?”

“Yeah. David Kendrick.”

Emily sighed. “Is he still going to school?”

“Who, you mean Trevor?”

“Yeah.”

“I think so. I don’t know. I have no idea, actually.” I gobbled the last bites of macaroni, gulped down my water, and rinsed out the bowl for the dishwasher. “If this guy is a weird ass, Emily, I want to keep an eye on Trevor. I don't want him getting involved with anything stupid." I didn't tell her that Chad's influence also concerned me.

I also didn't tell her I'd been snagged into the fold of David's promise of money just as much as Trevor and Chad. There was something about the whole enterprise that tempted me, and I wanted Emily to be, if not excited about it, at least intrigued by the possibilities of easy-to-attain cash for as long as David would allow it.

"Do what you want, Alex. I don't approve, but watching over your brother might not be a bad thing. Just be careful, okay?"

"Of course." I gave her a kiss on the top of her head. In two days I would know more about these so-called favors. If something seemed off at the cemetery on Thursday, it would be the last time we went out there to meet David Kendrick.

Chapter 4

Ten a.m. Wednesday. I was in my office reformulating a layout for the January edition of the new-products section of our radio-control catalog. Absorbed with the dilemma of which struggling vendor should get a quarter-page of ad space in a rapidly crowded six-page section, the sudden ringing of the phone made my heart jump. I cleared my throat, picked up the phone, and said, "Promotions, Alex Neitzel."

A saucy voice imitated my greeting. It was my brother, who had never called me at work before.

"What can I do for you?" I asked.

"Um, are you busy?"

"A little. What's going on?"

"I was just wondering about tomorrow. Do you think you want to go out there?"

"I do."

"Well then, would you be interested in going to dinner with me and Chad afterward? After our big score," he added with a laugh.

I knew "score" referred to the money David would be giving us, and for some reason, Trevor's cavalier attitude rubbed me the wrong way. Lowering my voice, I said, "Thanks for the invite, but I need to get home right after. You know, Emily and all."

"What? Emily can't subsist if you're not home by seven at the latest every evening?"

"You know what I mean, Trevor."

"How about we get dinner before we go then?"

"Some other time, okay? I've got a few errands to run before we meet David."

"Yeah, okay, I get it. You're a busy married guy and all. If you change your mind, though, we're thinking Della Colomba on Neil Street. We *adore* that place."

"All right, sounds good." I was anxious to get off the phone.

"What do you think David's next favor will be?"

I looked at the open Excel file on my computer screen and massaged my eyes. Discussing David's "favors" over the phone felt risky. "Hard to say. Hopefully something easy."

"Chad thinks we could milk this guy for all he's worth for a long time."

"Yeah, well, Chad worries me. I don't want *him* making

decisions for you and me or taking things into his own hands."

"Chad doesn't want to get involved in anything illegal any more than you do."

"We should just be on the same page is all."

"I know. We're not stupid, Alex."

"Good. Make sure Chad knows, too."

"He knows, Alex."

Trevor changed the subject by asking about my car. I told him it was in the shop overnight and I was picking it up this evening. He mentioned how funny it was that a broken belt had led us to such a strange encounter at the cemetery with David. As he was blathering on about it a colleague stepped into my office, eager to discuss something.

"I have to go," I told Trevor, cutting him off.

Trevor said he'd see me tomorrow. It turned out his phone call wasn't the only family surprise of the day.

"I'm inviting you over for dinner," my dad declared in the lobby, as I was leaving work.

"Dad. What are you doing here?" I was truly taken aback.

"Well, you know, you guys never invite your mom and me over," he quipped—and then something strange happened: his expression changed from normal to distraught in a matter of seconds. It started with a crimson color that enveloped his face, which transformed to a scrunched look, making him look older. His lips quivered and he began to cry.

"Hey, what is it? What's going on?" I put my arm around his shoulder and guided him out the door.

Once out in the parking lot, Dad shook his head from side to side in short, hard movements, indicating he didn't want to talk—or maybe he was too choked up to do so. I placed my hand on his shoulder, holding it there. Dad's hands were covering his face, and I heard him mumble something.

"What did you say?"

He removed his hands. "I said I haven't been this sad in ages."

"Tell me what's wrong, Dad."

He sniffed his nose. "Your mom has a pretty advanced case of breast cancer. It was caught late, so it's going to be a real scramble to beat it. She knows it, too. She's not pretending."

This set off more choking up and tears, though not as bad as before.

"Oh, boy," I said. Light snowflakes trickled from the sky, landing on my face like cold pinpricks.

"Yeah, it's tough news. But we'll fight it till she's better. Nothing else we can do."

"I'm so sorry, Dad." He seemed more composed now, maybe because he'd told me the news, gotten it off his chest.

"I called Emily and told her already. Hope you don't mind."

"Of course not. Did she have any advice?"

"She wants to talk to your mom about nutrition and that kind of stuff."

"Good." Emily was known as the health guru in our family.

"So I'm going to head home; glad I was able to catch you here. Your wife is cooking up something and bringing it over. Not sure what."

"Great."

"Emily said your car is in the shop and she's picking you up?"

"Yeah. She should be here soon."

"What happened to it?"

"Just a busted belt."

He nodded. "I could have fixed that for you."

"Yeah, I should have thought of that."

"Well, all right then. Just be yourself around your mom when you guys come over. We can talk about it, of course. You don't have to pretend like it's not happening or anything like that. She's trying to be positive, but I know it's killing her inside. Just be supportive."

I watched Dad pull out of the parking lot and remained outside, letting the snow fall on me, oblivious now to its chill. When Emily pulled up, she had to honk to get my attention.

"Trevor knows about it and a few of her close friends know," Dad said at dinner. He was sitting next to my mom, holding her hand.

We'd finished eating and the mood was somber.

"Trevor was a wreck," Mom said softly. "It hit him pretty hard."

The dark circles under her eyes and pained expression on her face conveyed the distress she was going through. A tender feeling for both my parents infiltrated me all at once, and I thought of our lives together as a family. Dad was a plumber and Mom had held different jobs over the years; together, they'd made sure Trevor and I never lacked for anything.

The plan was to begin chemotherapy soon. Mom had been given a strict new diet from her doctor, and I could tell by looking at her plate, which was filled with greens and eggplant, that Emily had fixed her meal accordingly. None of us had much of an appetite.

After dinner we watched TV, flipping through channels, trying to find something halfway decent. We settled on a romantic comedy called *Doc Hollywood* with Michael J. Fox, a movie I'd seen before and liked but couldn't stay interested in. Emily suggested we play euchre, but no one else could muster the enthusiasm.

Emily collapsed into my arms when we got home, and I hugged her tight. We shuffled to the kitchen, our arms locked around each other's waist, Emily's head against my shoulder.

"Your poor mom. I hate this."

Emily made me decaf coffee and started the dishwasher. "These next few months will be hell for her," she said, wiping the kitchen counter.

"I could buy her some books. You know, books on cancer. Or

maybe some self-help books on staying positive."

"That's sweet, but be careful with the cancer books. I know you're trying to help, but you don't want to be giving advice that might be counterintuitive to what her doctor is telling her. Sometimes all these natural cures and medicines don't mix well together.

"It's like all those pregnancy and health magazines and books we've been buying, you know? One thing says this, another says that. It's *exhausting*. She probably doesn't want a million people giving her advice."

"I'm still going to do some research on breast cancer."

Emily sipped her water. "I hate to bring this up, but this whole thing makes me think that it's all the more reason for us to have a baby. Can you imagine how ecstatic your mom would be? It might even lift her spirits enough to help her fully heal."

My wife wanted a baby more than anything, so I tried to be patient.

"I want to talk to a doctor about in-vitro," she said. "I think it's time. We've been trying and trying and it hasn't worked."

I sighed; it wasn't the first time she'd broached this subject. "In-vitro is not *in*expensive," I said. "Come on, I just found out about my mom having cancer. Do we have to discuss this now?"

"But don't you see? It's the perfect time *to* be talking about it. Think about it, Alex, how joyful your mom would be. There are no negatives here. The thought of being a grandma could potentially make her happy enough to beat her cancer—and don't laugh at me for saying that. It's been proven that a positive mood and a healthy sense of well-being can help cure illnesses. Or, on a much sadder note, she could, you know, die with the beautiful thought that she's leaving behind a grandchild."

Emily wasn't wrong. Mom would indeed be thrilled to be a grandma, even if it was in the latter stages of a dying life. But would she live long enough to see our newborn baby? The doctor hadn't given her a death sentence; all he'd said was that without treatment the end would come fast. *With* treatment, however, she had hope and probably added time, perhaps months and maybe even a much longer life if something miraculous happened. Time, which Emily and I had a knack for treating like an unending ocean that was always available to wade through, suddenly seemed like an enclosing noose, a pond instead of a vast sea.

"I'm trying to wrap my head around my mom right now, honey. Maybe we *can* explore in-vitro, but let's talk about it later. You know that I want a baby as bad as you."

"Come upstairs," she urged, enclosing my hand into hers. The kitchen was clean and the dishwasher was humming through its cycle, a lulling, pleasing sound.

"You go ahead. I'll be up soon."

I remained where I was, listening to the dishwasher, thinking about a baby and how it might indeed give my mom an added will to live.

Sleep didn't always come easy for me. It took me hours to drift off under the warm covers. I thought of my mom and her plight and the sorrowful demeanor of my dad, so unlike his usual state. I pondered Emily's idea to do in-vitro and thought about a meeting tomorrow at work that I wasn't looking forward to. I hated meetings.

But I was preoccupied most with something else: I was thinking about tomorrow evening with David Kendrick, wondering just how much money he had to spare.

Chapter 5

The throbbing guitar of "Every Breath You Take" filled the car as the three of us rode to the cemetery in silence. Trevor was especially quiet, and Chad seemed to be respectful of the solitude we both wanted. He knew about my mom, and the disheartening news I think added to the already tense vibe we were feeling about the uncertainty of David's next task.

As we rounded the circular path and made our way to the back of the cemetery, I noticed again how the headstones seemed to be splattered throughout in a random fashion, giving the grounds a ramshackle look. I wondered if the land was maxed out in its capacity to hold more coffins, and if so, how forlorn it would be when the people who visited the deceased on a regular basis also passed away. Who would come here then?

I could see David kicking stones in front of his car as we approached. He seemed taller than I remembered from a few days ago. We rolled to a stop and he greeted us like we were all the best of buddies.

"You made it!" he crowed. "I was worried you guys might skip out on me."

"We wouldn't do that," Trevor said.

"Let's get into my car and talk there," David said. "It's too cold to stand out here."

I glanced at Trevor and Chad. "Uh, if it's all the same with you, how about we talk outside."

David looked perplexed. "Are you sure?"

"You got us on pins and needles, man. What's your next task?" Chad asked.

David chuckled. "Boy, you guys are antsy. Where I come from, people get to know each other before getting down to business. What say we bond?"

David was staring at me, I guess hoping I'd make the call on whether it was okay or not to bond.

He laughed again. "Come on, relax, guys! We're here to get to know one another, become friends. That's your favor to me this evening, okay, just to talk. We can get into my car and get the heat cranked." David inhaled deeply, bucked his head upward, and stomped his foot. "It's too damned cold to talk out here."

"We're fine," I said. "Let's just get this over with."

“Well, okay, if you’d rather stand out in the cold and freeze to death. Tell me about yourselves then. You two. You guys partners or whatever you want to call it?”

Trevor and Chad looked at each other and laughed. “Yeah, we’re together,” Chad said. “Call it whatever you want, cowboy.”

Embarrassed, I shuffled my feet and veered my eyes downward.

“Hey, I got nothing against gay people,” David said. “My wife and I used to have this gay gardener who came over to the house to plant flowers and spruce up the vegetation in our yard. His name was Carl, and he was one of the nicest, most inventive guys I ever met. We used him for years till he moved down to Atlanta.”

Thus, the conversation was off and running. David inquired about each of us, and in turn, he opened up about himself, telling us about his memories in the worlds of medicine and business, where he’d made lots of money.

David was exceptional at something that I was not good at: telling stories. More than once he made the observation that “young kids” today had somehow forgotten about and missed out on the fine art of carrying on stimulating conversations. Was that true? Emily and I could often be the two quietest people in large groups, and the only time I ever opened up about anything was with her—and sometimes it felt like that wasn't too often.

At some point, Trevor made it known his toes were about to fall off because of the cold.

"How about we get into *your* car then to talk some more," David prodded, turning to me. "Since you don't trust me and all."

I chuckled. "This has been fun, but my wife is going to start getting worried. We should probably wrap it up."

"Aw, come on, just a little longer," David pleaded. He pulled out a mini flashlight and opened his winter jacket, shining it inside. "Look, I'm not carrying anything. Check my pockets." He yanked out the inner lining of his jacket pocket and the pockets of his pants to show they were empty.

He held the flashlight at his waist, shining it upward onto his face. I peered into his red-rimmed eyes, which had a worn-out look and baggy pouches beneath them. I could see he was telling the truth; David really did just want to talk some more.

"Okay, twenty minutes," I said, "and then we've got to go."

We piled into my car and I started up the car and revved the engine, trying to generate heat as fast as possible. David was in the front seat, and I'll never forget how we turned to look at one another at the exact same moment. His head seemed to be on a mechanical swivel as he looked at me—sort of like that freaky girl in *The Exorcist*—and I noticed his eyes had a maniacal edge to them.

"I want you to kill my wife," David said. "She's already half dead anyway, so you'd be doing her, and me, a big favor. That's God's honest truth."

I looked at Trevor in the rearview mirror. His mouth was agape. "Whether you say yes or no, I'll pay you each a thousand bucks tonight for our sparkling conversation," David continued. "You'll get five million tax-free dollars for the merciful dispensing of my wife, and a promise from me that you'll never get caught. Five million dollars split up three ways is close to one point seven million dollars, boys. That's a lot of bread for three young guys with their whole lives ahead of them."

My thoughts shifted to topnotch cancer treatment centers, affordable artificial insemination methods for getting Emily pregnant, and faraway islands that were always sunny. Life suddenly seemed bountiful. So when I heard the revulsion expressed in Trevor's response, I had a hard time comprehending what was bothering him so much.

"Come again?" David said, also taken aback by Trevor's outburst.

"I said get the hell out of the car." I'd never heard Trevor sound so riled up before—or frightened, for that matter.

"Settle down," I told him.

"Yeah, let's think this through," Chad said. "This guy just offered us five million freaking dollars—I want to hear what he has to say."

For a resentful moment, I was perturbed by how Chad also coveted the idea of so much money.

"I can't *believe* you guys!" Trevor shouted. "We're talking about murder here, and I'll have no part of it. I can't believe you're listening to, much less considering *doing*, this," he admonished. "This is just the type of thing we all three vowed to stay *away* from."

"Yes, Trevor, we know." I stayed silent for a moment and then blurted to David, "My mom was diagnosed with breast cancer. She found out recently, and it's pretty bad."

"*Our* mom!" Trevor yelled from the back seat.

"What a rotten deal," David said in a plaintive voice. "What's the prognosis?"

"Not great. I mean, ultimately, I don't think she has a lot of time left."

"Why are you telling this guy that, Alex? What the hell is *wrong* with you?" Trevor yelled, hitting the back of my seat with his hand as he did so.

Without looking back at him, I raised my hand upward in a sharp manner, as if I were a stern, stressed-out parent or a strict schoolteacher admonishing a misbehaving child with the mere flick of my arm.

"Oooh, what is that, big brother? Are you going to whip my behind or something if I speak out of turn again?" Trevor said.

"*If* we do this," Chad said, interrupting the family conflict, "and I'm not saying we are, but if we say yes, how would it happen? How would we … kill her?"

David turned in his seat so he could see all three of us. "'We' is the wrong word, my friend. I'm paying you and Trevor for just keeping quiet." He started coughing, forcing us to wait to hear what he'd say next. Finally, David continued: "It's Alex here who will do the deed, if he so chooses. And believe me, guys, it's foolproof. All very nice and tidy."

His words sounded heartless, but he'd roped me in—at least a little. "Okay, so tell us," I prodded. "How would you want me to do it, if I actually agree to do this crazy thing?" The casual manner in which I asked David how I'd potentially be killing his wife was a disturbing feeling.

"Phyllis is flat-out sick," David said. "Half the time she's knocked out on medication, and half the time she barely knows where—or who—she is. When she *does* come to her senses, she reviles me with an intensity that is downright scary."

David paused for a moment, and I observed this fact made him sad. "I've told you our marriage has been falling apart for decades, and now here I am, in my seventies, wanting to finally be single again so I can live out my days down in Florida in peace."

"If she's so sick, why don't you just wait it out, just wait for her to die?" Chad inquired.

"Like I said, I'm in my seventies. And as bad off as Phyllis is, she could live a long time yet. She's being cared for in our home, and that's another thing that grates on me to no end—the constant stream of nurses and care workers in my own house. It's never ending. I'm getting up there in age, and though it may sound selfish, I want to be able to do what *I* want to do. And my slowly dying wife is holding me back."

"Why didn't you just divorce her a long time ago?" I asked.

"Come on. Coulda, woulda, shoulda. How do you want me to answer that? You think we didn't discuss divorce or other options during all our years together? Our marriage became an arrangement after a while, pure and simple, but divorce was just something neither of us wanted to go through with, for reasons we had in common."

"Maybe you loved her and still do," Trevor said. "Maybe this killing idea is a terrible one."

To my surprise, David didn't brush this off. "Maybe so. Maybe I love her more than I'm letting on, and maybe I shouldn't kill her, but I'm still asking you to." David was looking at me.

"How did you guys meet?" I asked, wanting him to talk about his wife in a good light. The idea of offing her—even for loads of money—suddenly felt like something I wasn't capable of.

“It was so long ago. We met through mutual friends. Back when I was in my early twenties, there used to be what was known as ‘rooftop dancing’ atop the old Remington’s Department Store building in downtown Champaign. I’d met Phyllis two or three times before, and one night, with a group of friends, we were at a rooftop dance and she and I noticed each other more so than on those other previous encounters. Well, that’s not entirely true. Phyllis told me she’d wanted me to ask her out before that, but I honestly don’t recall her acting coquettish in any way. Then again, she wasn’t really coquettish by nature. Or maybe I just completely missed all the signals, who knows. Anyhow, the night of that dance when we finally did notice each other, it was—”

He stopped talking for a moment, I guess pondering the memory, and then resumed.

“I’m sorry to sound like a Hallmark card here, guys, but it was truly a special, magical night. We danced, we got mildly drunk from some liquor we’d snuck up there, and we ended up kissing at the end of the evening. Even today, as I recall it now, it ranks as one of the best nights—one of the best *times*—of my life. There it is, boys. Dating Phyllis in those early years was one of the best times of my life."

"And now you want her killed." Trevor said. "This is unbelievable."

David turned to look at Trevor. "I want to mercifully end her life, yes. Times change, young man. Circumstances change. *Life* changes. We'd be doing a great favor by putting her out of the misery that passes for her life. You don't know what it's like for her, or for me." David's voice was rising. "We live with all this money, and yet I live in a house of squalor where no one talks, the clocks all tick incessantly, and my longest conversations, which usually aren't all that long, are with the newest nurse covering the latest shift of my wife's slow death watch, which could drag on for years. It's no way to live, for either of us."

"Put her in a home and be done with it," Chad said. "That would solve your problem."

"It would, wouldn't it," David admitted. "Trouble is, I promised her long ago I wouldn't do that, and I can't break that pact. She doesn't want to live anywhere except her own home, and we have the means to make that happen. I've been hurtful enough to her in the past. That's the one promise I can't break."

"What's wrong with her?" I asked. "Is it cancer or something?"

"Leukemia that fluctuates between near death and a manageable state, arthritis, and a thousand other things that one human being should not have to endure."

David's demeanor reminded me of my dad's when he was relating the news about Mom's breast cancer. It was strange how such misery had pervaded my world in the space of a few days.

"So your wife hates you, and you want her dead because you probably still love a part of her, and you want to go to Florida? Am I hearing all this right?" Trevor asked.

"You're complicating things," David whispered.

"Trevor, ease up," I said.

We were all silent for a long moment. The heat in the car was becoming stifling, so I turned it down. When I piped up, I was surprised to find that I didn't continue the discussion about David's proposition.

"My wife and I, sometimes we have a hard time. When I think about five years down the road or whatever, I sometimes wonder what it'll be like. I mean, I wonder if we'll drift and eventually loathe each other. Like what happened with you and your wife."

"It shouldn't come to that, not if you work at it," David said.

But why, I wanted to ask him, did marriage have to be such *work*?

"Phyllis and I are an old-fashioned couple, in the sense that we carried on despite our problems. We never split up. These days it seems like couples divorce at the drop of a hat. You and your wife will either work it out or you'll get divorced, but I doubt you'll live in misery like we did for so many years. It's just not a good way to live."

"Look at Mom and Dad," Trevor said. "They weren't exactly happy campers for a long time, but they worked it out. You and Em will be fine. You were meant for one another."

I ignored him. My mood had darkened and I no longer felt like discussing money or marriage or anything else. I wanted to head home, so that's what I told everybody.

David seemed to understand that the timing was right to part ways. "Look, if I sicken you all and you never want to see or speak to me again, I understand. But please don't tell the authorities on me, okay? I haven't done anything yet, and I may never. I'm not a bad, evil guy who's looking to murder his wife and marry some bimbo down in Florida. It's not like that at all. All I want is peace and solitude, no sickness. And I want to quietly end a life that needs ending."

"Why don't you just do it yourself?" Trevor asked.

David stared straight ahead for more than ten seconds before answering. "I can't," he finally admitted. "Even though all it would take is one measly pill, I just can't do it myself."

I looked at him. "A pill? That's how you'd do it?"

"Yep. Just slip her a little untraceable pill that will do the job, end things for good."

"Why not have one of the nurses do it?" I asked.

"I thought about that really hard. There was one gal in particular who I thought might be up for the task, but then she moved on to somewhere else. I haven't had the guts to ask any of the other nurses. When this happens—*if* it happens, I should say—I'll be down in Florida. That'll be my alibi."

I gripped the steering wheel and looked down at my lap. "Try to have a good night," I told David.

David looked at me for a moment, caught off guard, I think, by the finality in my tone.

"I'll do that," he responded. "But please make your decision fast or I might be swallowing that little white pill myself." He opened the door and eased himself out of the car, slamming it in front of our surprised faces.

"Go ahead and do us a favor," Trevor said.

"Hey, what about the thousand bucks each he promised us for talking to him tonight!" Chad exclaimed.

"He never said how we can reach him," I said.

"Who cares," Trevor retorted. "Just let it go, you guys. He's crazy. It's like he lives in this stupid cemetery or something."

"He's not crazy," I countered. "He's just sad." I pushed the car door open and jogged toward David, yelling his name. I remembered how helpless he had seemed on the ground in the cemetery, when he'd slipped on the ice, and how strong he was about it afterward, as if the incident had been no big deal and he was intruding upon our time. I felt bad for what he was dealing with regarding his wife, and I told him that.

"Don't worry about me," David said, patting me on the shoulder. "I'll soldier on. And I understand if you don't want to end my wife's life. It was a bold request, and maybe I shouldn't have thrown it at you."

I looked down at my feet, thinking about the offer. "Would you really pay us five million dollars?"

"Yes. No strings attached." He looked me dead in the eyes and waited for a response.

"Well, do you have a way I can reach you?"

David looked around the area and said, "It would be wise if we didn't meet in public, and probably wiser still not to talk on the phone. I haven't seen a soul out here in this cemetery during the two times we've met, so I think this place might be our safest bet. Don't you?"

"I guess so."

"How much time do you need to make your decision?"

"How about two days."

"That works. So we'll meet here at the same time in two days then?"

"Yeah."

"If you say yes when we meet, I'll have the money here for you and give it to you then, okay? I'll give you all of it, because I trust you. And here, let me give you the money I owe you guys for tonight. I forgot all about that earlier," he said, reaching into his back pocket.

I moved myself in front of David so Trevor and Chad couldn't see him. "No, that won't be necessary. We all agreed we don't want it. Thanks anyway, though."

"Are you sure?"

"Yeah. I'll see you in a few days." I hustled back to the car, feeling better and more in control of things.

"What were you guys talking about?" Chad asked as I was putting on my seatbelt.

I eyed him in the rearview mirror. Trevor was still back there with him, probably because he was angry and didn't want to sit up front with me.

"I told him no, and I told him we wouldn't be back, Chad. I told him we all three decided it wasn't a good idea to get involved, but that we wish he and his wife the best."

Chapter 6

The following evening, I was watching an entertaining movie on cable, *Hard Eight*, when the doorbell rang.

"Who could that be?" Emily said from the kitchen.

"Dunno," I mumbled from the couch, pulling myself up with reluctance. I walked to the front door, flipped on the porch light, and was surprised to see Trevor standing there, a hangdog look on his thin face. He had his hair slicked back with gel, giving him a stylish, more kept look.

"Hi. Am I disturbing you and Emily during dinner?" he asked.

"No, we haven't eaten yet but are going to. I'm watching a really good movie. Come on in and you can watch it with me."

"Wait," he said, startling me. Trevor inched nearer and whispered, "I want to talk to you about last night."

I looked behind me to see if Emily was watching, and then I slipped outside the door. "How'd you get here?"

"The bus, like usual." He scuffed his shoes on the concrete and cleared his throat. "Does David remind you of Grandpa Lenny?"

I chuckled, right away recognizing the similarities. "He does, actually. Maybe that's why I feel this weird connection to him."

Trevor studied me, narrowing his eyes. “Yeah, I can see that you do.”

“What? Do you disapprove?”

“I can just tell you like him, that’s all. Just like you were crazy about Grandpa Lenny when he was alive. Your eyes would light up like a Christmas tree when he came into a room. I remember.”

My mom had told me over the years how enamored I was with her father, especially when I was young. “So you think I’m having grandpa flashbacks or something like that?”

“Maybe subconsciously. I also think you were seriously contemplating David’s offer last night, at least for a minute.”

“I told you guys, Trevor. I cut it off with David. None of us will be getting that money.”

Looking peeved, Trevor said, “It’s not exclusively your call. Chad or I could do the deed, if we could convince David. For some reason he thought only *you* were capable of doing it.”

“Trevor—”

“Chad and I won’t be together forever, you know.”

This surprised me. “Uh, okay. What does that have to do—?”

"You and I could split the money, just between us. Keep him out of it."

"I don't understand. I thought you liked Chad."

"We have a good time, but he's not my forever guy by any means. David's money gets me much more excited."

I couldn't help but laugh. "Wait a second. Last night you were totally against this, and now you're all psyched about getting his money. What's changed?"

Trevor pressed his lips together and a thoughtful look came over his face. "I feel sorry for him, for one thing. And for her; his wife. Their life *does* sound awful. If you could get in there and slip her a mercy pill ... maybe it wouldn't be such a bad thing."

The front door opened, alarming me. Emily popped her head out and asked Trevor if he was staying for dinner.

"Oh, well, sure, if you don't mind."

"Good, then come inside, guys. Let's eat." Emily looked at me and said, "Or do you need more time?"

"No, we'll be right in."

Emily closed the door and Trevor said, "I guess we can talk about this later." He reached for the doorknob, but I pulled his elbow toward my stomach, preventing him from going inside. "Hold on a second. I wasn't totally honest with you, Trevor."

He tilted his head and gave me a curious look. "Okay. What's up?"

"After I jumped out of the car to talk to David last night, right before we left, we made plans to meet again."

"I knew something was up with that conversation!"

"Shh, keep it down. I told him I'd think about doing the deed, but now, talking here with you, I think I want to do it for sure." I leaned in close to him. "It's like you said, Trevor, we could split up the money, fifty-fifty, just you and me."

Trevor nodded and smiled. "All right."

"All right. So maybe it would be best if you ended things with Chad as soon as possible."

"God, do you know what this means? We'll be *so* set for life!"

"Not so loud, Trevor. Did you hear what I said just now about Chad? You need to end it with him, but let him down easy."

"Okay, okay."

"And yes, you're right—we will have a lot of money, but I hope you realize it's going to cause us a whole different set of problems once it's ours. I mean, we're going to have to be as inconspicuous as possible around town. We can't just go around flaunting our cash. Maybe some of it could go toward helping Mom. "

Trevor didn't seem to hear me. "Life will be *so* much different," he said in a dreamy way. "How are we going to tell Mom and Dad? Or *are* we going to tell them?"

"Are you out of your mind? Of *course* we're not going to tell Mom and Dad. Listen, you just need to focus on Chad, okay? Try to get him out of your life in a, you know, a nice way if you can."

"You already said that, Alex."

"And *please* don't bring any of this up during dinner, okay? Emily knows a little bit about David, but not about the millions he offered us."

"When are you going to tell her?"

"When the timing is right, but definitely not now. Definitely not tonight."

For some reason, our dinner conversation lagged. For all that was on my mind—my mom's cancer, Emily's intense desire to have a baby, issues at work, whether or not I should accept five million tax-free dollars for performing a questionable act—all that I cared about at the moment was having a convivial meal with two close people in my world. And it wasn't happening.

Emily broached the subject of Mom's breast cancer to Trevor, who turned sullen and didn't have much to say. Trevor asked Emily what book she was reading, which, as luck would have it, was nothing at the moment. These and a few other topics saw the light of day and fizzled without a trace, when it hit me all of the sudden that Emily had just been given a bottle of wine for her recent birthday. When I announced that we were popping it open, I was pleased to see the looks of appreciation on both of their faces.

After finishing the first bottle, Emily suggested we open another. The mood and conversation had become livelier, as rosy as our pinkening faces.

"Ah, yes!" Trevor proclaimed, as I pulled out the cork from bottle number two, his pinched cheeks flushed with drink. "Chardonnay. A personal favorite of mine."

"Us too!" Emily exclaimed.

"When I'm a rich young man!" Trevor roared, "I shall roam and conquer the country and world drinking only Chardonnay to my heart's content."

Emily let out a playful laugh and played along. "And do you plan on being rich any time soon, you medieval knight in shining armor? Because if so, perhaps you could share your riches with us."

Trevor leaned in and grabbed Emily's hand, peering into her eyes. "Why, yes, fair lady, the riches shall be shared by all. Family is family, of course." He gave me a sly look, one that could have only been construed by Emily as being sneaky, even smarmy.

"Are you two drunks ready for brownies?" I asked. "Or maybe some coffee?"

"Coffee shmoffee," Trevor said, irritated at the suggestion while he was getting loaded. "Unless those brownies are laced with marijuana, I'm having laughs with your wife and drinking more wine."

Wine it is, I thought to myself.

"Pour me another glass, sweetie," Emily requested. "And bring me over a brownie. A marijuana brownie."

The two of them howled with laughter, making me realize the

wine was having the opposite effect on me; for whatever reason, a more solemn, even guarded, mood had enveloped me. But I smiled gamely and brought them over the whole plate of brownies. "Get as high as you want on these babies," I said, making them scream with laughter at my lame joke.

When the hilarity died down, Trevor asked us if he could smoke. After admonishing him about the habit, Emily gave him an ashtray from our cabinet and told him to smoke in the garage.

We played three-man euchre and drank some more, though I cut myself off by the third game. A wine-sodden sluggishness had clouded my thoughts and slowed my demeanor, and I noticed Emily was also losing steam. Still, it was good to have Trevor at our house. It was a Friday night, and for Emily and I, this was as wild as things usually got. Trevor and Emily kept repeating how we should do stuff like this more often.

Things faded by eleven o'clock, though Trevor wanted to play cards and drink some more. Emily began to clean up in the kitchen and family room, a hint that the party was winding down. Trevor rose to use the bathroom, and I noticed he was swerving unsteadily on his feet.

"I gotta get home," he slurred to Emily when he returned from the bathroom.

"Oh, no!" Emily responded with drunken, maternal forcefulness. "You're staying in our guestroom tonight. You're too wasted to be leaving."

Trevor gave in without a fight, and I walked next to him up the stairs, my left arm around his waist. Upstairs, Emily and I prepared his room for the night as he watched us in a grinning stupor. After making sure Trevor had everything he needed, Emily gave him a long hug, then kidded him about getting her so drunk and high on fake-pot brownies. Then she said goodnight, leaving us alone.

"I'm sorry," Trevor said after she left, sounding dejected.

"Sorry? For what? You didn't do anything wrong. We had fun tonight. Didn't you?"

"Yeah, it was fun," he said, his voice ragged. Trevor leaned back onto the bed, stretched out his arms and legs, and slipped off his shoes. The cigarette smell coming from his clothes was overpowering. I urged him to take them off and get under the covers, but he didn't seem to hear me.

"Do you remember when you moved out of Mom and Dad's house and I moved into your bedroom upstairs?" he asked me.

"Yeah, I remember. You loved that room. You really made it your own living area, too. It was like it was your own little apartment up there."

His eyes were closed and he was smiling. "You're right, I did make it my own. When all the lights in the room were out at night, there used to be a beam that came in through the window. It filtered through the blinds and illuminated on the wall in the shape of a cross."

I stood above him, not sure where he was going with this, but curious. "You mean, like, *the* cross?" I asked.

"That's right, the Jesus Christ cross. It made me feel really good every single night. Protected, I guess you could say."

Trevor stopped talking for a second, and I thought he was going to fade out entirely. I sat down on the bed and said, "Go on. Tell me more about the cross."

He opened his eyes, looking somewhat discombobulated. "Well, later on, my cross changed. Maybe it was the neighbor's outside light doing something different, or maybe my blinds shifted, or maybe the darkness of night or my imagination was playing tricks on me, because at some point the cross lost its horizontal section. It became a one-stand cross. And even though it was broken or whatever, now just basically a stick, I still liked it. I liked it even more, in fact."

"A one-stand cross," I said, liking how that sounded.

"A stick, Alex."

He was fading fast. "Trevor, why did you joke with Emily during dinner about being rich someday? That wasn't a very prudent way to act."

He didn't answer me.

"Trevor?"

"I don't know. It seemed like a fun thing to do at the time. She didn't catch on to anything. Don't you care about my stick story?"

I did care about his story and wondered if maybe, just maybe, if we got that five million bucks, perhaps Trevor, Emily, and I could indeed travel the world like he'd said, drinking Chardonnay, moving on to different spots and experiencing things we'd never dreamed of—all the while taking care of each other. Em and I, in fact, could watch over Trevor as if he were our own—our son.

Trevor cracked open a suspicious eye. "What are you looking at? Are you trying to say you love me with those pretty brown eyes?"

"Sorry," I mumbled, reaching down to offer him a clumsy hug. Trevor patted me on the back, seeming to know it wasn't a natural act for me.

"I liked your cross story, Trevor. I really did."

"Stick story," he whispered.

I stood up and watched him for a few more moments and then shut off the light. Before closing the door I said goodnight, but I didn't get a response. Trevor was already asleep and snoring, so I turned him on his side and tiptoed to the door, shutting it quietly.

Emily was waiting for me underneath the covers, wearing nothing but skimpy panties and a diamond necklace that I'd gotten for her before we were married. I took off all my clothes.

"I *love* that your brother came over tonight," she purred. "It was fun."

"It was fun," I said, jumping in bed and caressing her leg.

“He was really on top of the world there for a minute during dinner, talking about traveling and all that. I wish he’d just get his associate’s degree and find a good job. Do you think he’ll ever get his degree?”

“He might.” I curled up next to her smooth skin and absorbed the body heat that radiated, rubbing her legs and then stomach in a circular motion, movements that turned her on.

“He drinks like that and he starts getting grand visions,” Emily said.

I turned and leaned my head on the pillow, thinking. Dreams of a financially improved life acquired via illicit money was a dangerous way to live, and I now felt foolish for thinking that Trevor could travel the world with Emily and I—or that he would even want to. The silly notion likely stemmed from the remnants of the alcohol I’d drunk earlier, nothing more than far-reaching, sentimental feelings toward my brother and a misplaced hope that we’d all be together forever.

Trevor was his own man, and it occurred to me all of the sudden that if anyone could be lavish to the point of recklessness with two point five million dollars, it would be him. I recalled his drunk-driving accident a few years ago. If we went through with helping David, a sit-down with my brother was going to be necessary to convey how careful we all three needed to be with the money: him, me, and Emily.

Beneath the covers, Emily was feeling me in spots too, making me forget about Trevor, Chad, and the money. I kissed her mouth and cheeks with woozy passion and eased a finger inside her, listening to her moan in the soft way I liked. Miles away a train was blaring its hazy-sounding horn in the cold night, not a disturbing noise at all, but rather, a dramatic, faraway reverberation that enhanced the romantic aura as my wife and I gathered steam to make love.

I climbed above her and we began, slow at first and then much faster and harder, almost frantic. I'd not been buzzed like this in a while, and whenever I was in this state our lovemaking could go on for a while. We were loud but also conscious of unconscious Trevor, a curious mix of devil-may-care drunkenness mixed with cautious familial love that paved the way toward our final throes.

"Get me pregnant," Emily whispered in a sexy voice, pressing her nails into my back, hard.

We would find out later that Emily got her wish. But for now, we climaxed and cried out together, lost in the moment. Not long afterward, as we held each other, spent, I couldn't help but feel like this was the foreboding prologue, an introduction preceding a nightmare of some dreadful unraveling.

And then I thought of Trevor's "stick story" and drifted off to sleep.

Chapter 7

Emily wasn't beside me when I woke up the next morning, which was unusual; usually I rose earlier than her. I could smell cooked bacon wafting up the stairs, blanketing me with familiarity and warmth. The thought of a bacon, egg, and cheese sandwich made my mouth water. I stretched, glad it was Saturday and content I was married to such a kind, beautiful woman. Why had I complained to David that marriage was a lot of work?

My timing was perfect when I walked into the kitchen—breakfast was ready.

"Grab a plate," Emily said, heading to the kitchen counter with her own plate of food. "The English muffins are in the toaster if you want to toast them for a sandwich."

I kissed her cheek. "You read my mind. Are you feeling okay?"

"Yeah, I'm good. I drank some water last night to stay hydrated."

"Good thinking. I wonder how Trevor will be feeling. He hit it harder than we did."

"He's gone already, but he left a note."

"I thought for sure he'd sleep in today."

“He told me last night he had to work early. I offered to give him a ride home this morning, but he said he’d take the bus. Oh, by the way, are you guys doing something tonight?”

I turned around from the toaster to look at her. “Tonight? No, I don’t think so. Why?”

“Here.” She handed me a slip of paper with Trevor’s scrawl:

Hey bro,

Come by tonight and we’ll head out there.

L8TR,

Trev

“Oh, yeah, I remember now. He kept asking me if I’d take him out driving on a country road. You know, for driving practice to get his license back.”

“I don’t remember you guys talking about that.”

“It was in the guest bedroom, after you went to bed. He mentioned wanting to practice driving to get back into the swing of things.”

Emily split apart a piece of bacon, holding the separated pieces in each hand. “Don’t get caught. I’d hate to see him get in trouble for driving without a license.”

I crumpled up the note and tossed it in the garbage can.

Trevor worked at the public library, so I went there after breakfast. I told Emily I was heading to the office to do some work and would be back in an hour. Lie number two for the day.

Trevor was shelving DVDs when I arrived, reading something on one of the boxes when I walked up to him.

"That note you wrote this morning wasn't smart," I said, catching him by surprise.

Trevor pondered my statement for a moment and then, in a miserable tone, said, "Give me a break. I'm hungover."

He sounded melancholy, but I didn't care. He'd pissed me off. "Why did you leave a note that says we have plans tonight? I had to lie to Emily and say I was giving you a driving lesson so you could get your license back. I hate lying to Emily."

"A driving lesson?"

"Yeah. I didn't know what else to say."

"Well, you would have had to lie to her anyway since we're going to the cemetery tonight to meet David. I guess saying you were going to help me practice driving was as good an excuse as any."

"Wait, I don't recall us talking about you going with me to meet David tonight."

"Oh, okay. Well, go yourself then. I feel like shit anyway."

"Look, Trevor, I'm mad that you left a stupid note that let Emily know we're going to be doing something tonight. It's not smart, and we have to be smart about things. Can't you understand that?"

"Yes, fine, point taken. I'm sorry."

"What about Chad? Has he talked to you about the other night?"

Trevor shoved a DVD onto the shelf, hard. "He's in Chicago this weekend. I wish you'd quit harping on him. He's not going to be an issue, okay? He thinks the whole thing with David was a weird encounter, a waste of time." Trevor grabbed another DVD and this time slid it in gently between two others.

"Do you have to shelve those alphabetically?" I asked.

"Of course. Do you want to borrow a knife for tonight?"

I looked around to make sure no one could hear our conversation. "Why would I want a knife, Trevor?"

"In case David turns out to be whacko."

"Dude, you're being weird. I'll be fine." I swiped a DVD off the cart and read the title—*Lake Placid.* The jaws of what looked to be a crazy crocodile were wide open, dripping with water and ready to snap shut, make the kill. "This was horrible," I said, flipping the case back onto the cart.

"It was kind of fun in a campy, B movie sort of way. Lots of blood and guts, I remember that much about it."

"Blood-and-guts-type movies are the worst kind. They never have a good plot, you know?"

Trevor pursed his lips. "That's a bit of a generalization. Listen, you need to get going. I have lots of work to do. Let me know if you change your mind and want me to go with tonight."

"Thanks, but you won't have to. It'll be fast and there's no need for you to be there," I said, walking away from him.

"I can't wait to see all that money."

I kept walking, pretending I hadn't heard what he said.

We needed light bulbs and a few other household supplies, so I told Emily I was heading to Home Depot that evening; it was a logical excuse to leave the house and she had no qualms. I knew she'd be content to stay home and grade papers, maybe catch up on some magazines. I kissed her on the cheek, told her I loved her, and headed out.

Trevor's suggestion about bringing a knife for protection had jolted me a little, so I slipped my pocket knife into the pocket of my khakis. It'd be useless if David had a gun, but it made me feel a little better having it, just in case he turned out to be a crazy killer, like Trevor had said.

David was not at our spot in the cemetery when I arrived, and his absence made me edgy, worried that he wouldn't show. What if David had lost his nerve to do this? It bummed me out to think of Emily and I living our lives without the money, not getting the chance to have the extraordinary future I had in mind, a life she knew nothing about at this point.

It struck me all of the sudden just how much I wanted this loot. The idea of *not* having it, in fact, made me feel bitter, like I'd been cheated and the future was pointless. I snapped off the car radio, folded my arms across my chest, and peered outward for signs of David's headlights coming in off U.S. 150.

He showed up fifteen minutes later. I plastered on my best smile and stepped out of the car to greet him. “Hey there! I was beginning to wonder if you were going to show.”

“Sorry. Phyllis is in particularly bad shape tonight. Kind of slowed me down. Plus I’m not feeling all that well.”

“Oh, sorry to hear that.”

David had brought a flashlight and turned it on. His face looked as if it had aged even from just a few days ago. He looked wan, wrinkled, and haggard. I placed my hand on his shoulder and gave it a light shake, an act of camaraderie. “I’ve decided I’ll do it, David.”

He smiled and said, “Good. Okay then.”

David used his key to pop open the trunk; inside was a large gray suitcase. He flipped up two gold latches on top and, voila—there the money sat: six neat rows of stacked and bundled one hundred dollar bills. I pried one bundle of bills out—it wasn’t easy to do since they were so jammed in together—and flipped through one end of the paper to the other with my thumb as if it were a paperback book. I whistled, not knowing what else to do or say. The promised money was right in front of me, and I was transfixed.

“Do you want to count it?” David asked.

“I don’t know. It seems like that would take an awful long time. Hey, do you have a cold? You don’t sound so great.”

“Just a little stuffed up. It wouldn’t be like counting to ten, but for my own peace of mind, I’d like to count it together. I don’t want to hear from you later on that the money wasn’t all there. Let’s do this right.”

So we lifted the heavy suitcase from the trunk, eased it onto the frozen ground, and counted the packets next to the flashlight. The more we counted, the more stupefied I became over just how rich of a man I now was. The sheer number of packets within the suitcase’s deep interior was stunning; counting the money was an enjoyable, eye-opening exercise, and I soon lost track of time.

I was never much good with numbers in school, so over the years I’d learned on my own and on the fly how to track personal finances, maintain a steady budget, and spend within the allotted amount of money I earned each month and year. Money had never retained a powerful hold over me, and I’d always considered myself to be someone who was able to subsist in a rather minimalist fashion. But handling this much bread had an empowering effect. Seeing all the packets, I felt as if I hadn’t wanted enough for myself and for Emily over the years. But we *did* deserve more, it seemed to me, and now we would have more.

When we finished counting and the five million dollars was tucked safely back into the suitcase, I knew we'd now have to talk about my end of the bargain. The enormous amount of cash was all there, but the devious task ahead of me sapped the warm and fuzzy feelings I had toward the money like a vacuum. In order for this large suitcase to be all mine with no strings attached, I knew what had to be done. Part of me wondered if I could somehow slip the blade of my little pocket knife into David's jugular and speed away, not having to worry about killing his wife or being connected to him.

What was I becoming?

"Now, here's the pill you'll give Phyllis in three days at six p.m. sharp," David informed me.

He handed me a sandwich bag with one white pill inside. It was hard to believe such a small thing could kill someone, but I didn't question him. I put the bag in my pocket and waited for him to continue.

"Here's my address and the date and time you're supposed to do this," he said, handing me a piece of paper. "Our house is in Mahomet, and it's easy to get to. Just take—"

"That's okay," I interrupted, holding up my hand. "I can look up the directions online."

He looked at me for a second and then said, "Okay then. Like I said, come by at six p.m. There's a side door on the east side of the house that's secluded and lets you into the garage and then into the house. My wife is on the first floor in the family room. You'll see her right away when you walk in; it'll be well lit. Don't turn any lamps or lights on or off; leave everything the way it is. You're going to have a window of time before the night nurse arrives, but don't waste any time. Just get in and out as fast as you can."

"What's my window of time?"

"About an hour."

This made me nervous. "What if she comes early? Or what if the other nurse is still there?"

"Don't worry, Alex. These nurses always adhere to the same schedule every day. They know I'll be out of town for a few days, and they know there will be periods when Phyllis is by herself, very short periods. It's going to be okay. You'll have enough time to do what you need to do and get out of the house unseen."

"All right."

"Now, the pill I gave you works fast and is tasteless. Make sure she drinks the entire glass of water that I'll leave by the side of the bed. Tilt her head backwards so she swallows it down, and make sure you wear latex gloves the whole time."

"Okay, yeah. Latex gloves. Good idea."

David had another coughing fit, similar to the one he'd had the other day in the car. When he regained his composure, he said, "And make sure to park at the end of the dead-end street, which is where my house is. It's dark and secluded and no one will be able to make out your car there."

An overwhelming nervousness had overtaken me. Maybe killing this guy *would* be the best option.

"You know I'll be in Florida by the time you do this thing, right?" he asked.

"Yeah, I remember you saying that."

He tilted his head in a quizzical way. "You *are* going to do this, aren't you?"

"Of course I am."

"Good, because I know who you are and will be able to retrieve the money from you quicker than you even knew you had it. Trust me on that, Alex."

"You won't have to do that. Consider it done."

"Good, I *will* consider it done. Now, let's move this behemoth to the trunk of your car and get the hell out of here."

All at once David repulsed me, and a shot of courage ran through my veins.

We straddled both sides of the large suitcase and lifted. Prior to that David had counted off "One, two, three!" … the final words of his life. My end of the suitcase was up, but David had toppled forward, a gigantic, sickening wheeze escaping his throat, as if he had severe asthma. I dropped the suitcase and, startled, stepped back and observed him writhing on the ground, his hands clutching his heart. David's eyes bulged and he looked at me in a state of shock, as if I were the one who'd caused his current state. His agony lasted for perhaps thirty or forty seconds, and then he stopped moving. I stood near him, feeling guilty.

I knew CPR and could have tried to help him.

I stepped forward and crouched down, putting my ear next to his mouth, listening for a breath and hearing nothing. I stood back up, smiling.

What a lucky break!

I grabbed the flashlight off the ground and yanked the suitcase up, my adrenaline helping me slide its bulky weight across the hard ground and onto the lip of the trunk of my car, where it teetered and almost fell backward. Panting and feeling the biting cold nipping at my ears, I gave it a shove. It slid into the trunk with a thud.

I scanned the cemetery, making sure no one was around. David was sprawled on the ground, not far from his son's grave, with one hand over his heart; the other hand must have slipped off. It felt strange that I would always be the person who knew about his death before anyone else, and that I was not telling anyone about it. By the time the cops found him, his body would be rock hard due to the cold. They would decipher that the poor guy had died while visiting his son's grave, just an old man who'd met his end by the common cause of cardiac arrest.

As I was about to get in the car and leave, I had a sensation come over me that something wasn't right.

And that's when it hit me that I knew I was being watched. I whirled around and was shocked to see a slender, light-brown coyote glaring at me from ten feet away, its wolfish eyes somehow accusatory. The thing opened its mouth at full length and bared its razor-sharp teeth, then proceeded to take two steps toward me and howl into the moonless night.

I was caught off guard but had heard that these rat-like things were skittish. I snatched up a nearby rock and flung it as hard as I could. The stone struck it square on its right forepaw, and it let out a deep bark that contrasted with the shrill howl I'd just heard. I laughed at the dumb thing. The coyote now seemed less sure of itself, so I took advantage of the situation by pounding a menacing footstep toward it to show it the tables had turned—I was now the one on the attack. The animal limped away, its arrow-shaped head turned downward in shame.

Satisfied, I turned and climbed into my car. Above the rattle of the engine, I could hear the skinny coyote howling a pained wail into the cold night.

I drove the speed limit the whole way home, perturbed that I had no bags in my possession that held new light bulbs or any other household goodies. On the off chance that Emily noticed, I'd tell her they were in the car and that I'd get them in the morning. I'd probably have to go to Home Depot for real soon to get the actual items, but it was hardly a big deal—I was five million dollars richer and ecstatic about it.

As large, heavy snowflakes began cascading onto my windshield, I marveled again at the good luck I'd experienced at the cemetery. David keeling over with a heart attack had been a lucky thing. Already, though, I was concerned about how hard it would be to tell Emily about the massive amount of money that had come into our lives like a Christmas miracle. I feared she would disapprove of it, and the thought was dispiriting.

Another irritating thought was also harboring in the back of my mind, generating yet more anxiety: I realized that splitting up and sharing the money with Trevor was not going to be as easy as I'd first imagined it would be.

Chapter 8

The next morning, I awoke to see a grayish light seeping through the blinds of our bedroom window. I thought of the snow falling on the windshield on the way home last night and wondered how much of it may have accumulated.

As if reading my thoughts, Emily bounded in from the steamy, fresh-smelling bathroom, her wet hair plastered to her head, a big white towel hugging her body. "It snowed like crazy last night. I think we got like nine inches or something. We might be trapped inside all day." She seemed giddy with excitement.

I lunged from the bed just as she sat down on it, excited myself about seeing the first big snowfall of December—and content that David was concealed within it.

I tugged at the cord of the blinds to pull them up and saw an all-white view with snow piled high everywhere, and flakes still coming down. There didn't appear to be any wind, so the atmosphere looked and felt muffled, silent. The thought of David buried in an out-of-the-way cemetery under a mound of snow made me secretly joyous. Unless anyone close to David knew that he visited his son's grave every so often, my guess was that it could take several days before he was found, though his car might get discovered first.

After work the following day, I sat in the dining room of my parents' house with Emily, my dad, and Trevor. Dad had invited us over for dinner, wanting to provide an in-person update on Mom, who was sleeping in their bedroom.

"She's struggling with the chemo," Dad informed us, his elbows on the table, his hands clasped in front of his face as if he were praying. He picked at his plate of rotisserie chicken and rice, and I observed his haggard look—similar to David's appearance prior to keeling over and dying. "She's being as positive as she can, but it's hard for her," Dad continued, his lips trembling.

I reached over to put my hand on his shoulder. "Are you

satisfied with the care she's getting, Dad?"

From my peripheral view, I could feel Trevor looking at me. He had burst into my parents' house tonight a half hour after me, running late because of an overlong shift at the library. We hadn't had a chance to talk about the money that was now in my possession.

Dad perked up at my question. "Oh, yeah. The Kayle physicians are first rate, and so are the facilities. Kayle is one of the best places in the Midwest for breast cancer—it has its own breast cancer wing that's nationally respected. There's no problem in that regard."

That relieved me. Tucked away deep down in a place I hated, I was glad none of my new riches would have to be plundered for Mom's treatment. I recalled that not long ago I had *wanted* to help Mom with the money we'd stumbled into. What had made me so much more covetous since then? I hadn't even bothered to do any research on breast cancer, like I'd told Emily I wanted to do.

“That’s good,” I said to my dad. “But if you guys need help, tell us. We can assist financially if it comes down to that.”

Emily turned to look at me, probably wondering how, exactly, we could help in that regard.

Dad nodded and said he was lucky to have such caring kids.

After dinner we visited Mom, who had been in and out of sleep most of the day. A kerchief was wrapped around her balding head, which looked small. Later she’d get a wig, Dad had told us, after the first round of chemotherapy, but for now this would do. Her face was ghost white and she had dark rings underneath her eyes; they were mere slits when she opened them and focused in on us in a chemical daze.

“Hi there,” Emily said, taking a seat on the bed and stroking her hand.

I noticed Trevor was tearing up. Dad did most of the talking, telling Mom about dinner and what wonderful kids they had, Emily included. But conversation was minimal. We each gave her parting hugs and kisses and filed out of the room. Everyone except Dad.

With Dad in the bedroom and Emily cleaning up in the kitchen, Trevor and I snuck off. He asked me to go outside with him so he could smoke a cigarette.

Under the glare of the porch light, I could see that Trevor looked drained. His eyes were bloated and red from crying, and when I told him he needed to stop smoking, all he could say in a deadpan voice was, “Smoking is one of the few things in life that gives me pleasure right now.” I let it go.

“Unless,” he continued, in a brighter tone, “you give me some good news about the other night. Did you get the money?”

“I did get it.”

“Wow. What does five million dollars look like?”

“You have to see it to believe it.”

Trevor let out a whistle. “I hope I *do* get to see it soon. So when do you do the thing with his wife?”

I started to answer him and then stopped, unsure of what to

say.

But it was okay—Trevor was sympathetic to my situation. He held up his hand and said, "Wait, I'm sorry, don't tell me the details. I'm sure it's something you don't want to talk about."

"Thanks."

Trevor took a deep drag on his cigarette, staring at me with squinty eyes. He tilted his head up and blew out the smoke. "The important thing is we got the money. Right?"

"Right."

"David will get his wish for a more peaceful life, and his poor wife can finally have some peace herself."

"Listen, about the money, I have to tell you I'm not so eager to just split it up and start spending it right away. You know what I mean?"

Trevor tapped his cigarette and I watched as smoldering ashes sailed down, seasoning the snow on the sidewalk like pepper. "Well, no, not right away. But when do you want to split it up?"

"I want to wait until a reasonable amount of time has passed, just to make sure no one's knocking on our doors, asking questions."

"Yeah, that's cool."

"Good. We'll both be rich soon enough. A little more time isn't going to matter."

"But can you float me some? Maybe like a thousand or so?"

"Come on, Trevor, can't you wait? We're talking about millions of dollars here."

"Right, exactly, Alex. So what's a measly thousand dollars going to matter? I just want to pay off a few bills and some credit card debt. What's the harm?"

"The harm is that *I'm* the one putting my neck on the line here. We have to be careful, Trevor."

"You keep saying that!" he yelled, raising his hands in exasperation. "How is paying off a few bills being reckless?"

I shoved him, making him fall backward. He landed hard on his back.

Trevor looked up at me from the ground, a hurt expression on his face. “Owww,” he whined, and then he started coughing. He rose slowly, dusting off his behind, seeming subdued. “Shit,” he croaked, coughing some more and stamping out his cigarette on the ground. “Fine. I’ll leave you alone about it,” he said.

“You were being too loud.”

“So you had to push me?”

“Sorry, I shouldn’t have. I’ve been feeling so stressed lately.”

“Whatever. I can wait on the money. Whenever you’re ready to split it up is fine.”

If Trevor found out that David had suffered a fatal heart attack in the cemetery and that his wife was still living, he’d definitely have some questions. I wondered, all of the sudden, if it wouldn’t be a bad idea to give Trevor enough cash so he could take a trip somewhere, ensuring he wouldn’t hear any local news about David’s heart attack.

“Listen, let’s meet for lunch tomorrow at Moon Café at noon. I’ll give you a thousand bucks. Hell, I’ll give you two thousand.”

This made us friends again. “Really! Thank you!”

"Sure. Why don't you use the money to take a little trip? I mean, nothing extravagant, just a nearby getaway so you can relax."

"Eh, now's not the best time. I've got a bunch of shifts at the library. They need some notice."

"Listen, Trevor, family stuff aside, let's stop meeting and talking for a while, okay? Just until things with David and his wife blow over. We don't need to be arousing suspicion. Definitely don't get a hold of me by phone. You know how they can track things like that."

"Aw, that's a bummer," Trevor groused. "I just got a cool new smartphone that's got all these awesome features."

The following day, prior to my lunch with Trevor, I drove out to the cemetery to have a look. I wanted to see if there was any activity, perhaps a police car or an ambulance, maybe official police tape lining the area or a few detectives surveying the scene, taking notes and talking into recorders.

But there was nothing of the sort. Instead, I observed a yellow siren that gave me a momentary flash of panic—until I realized it was a snowplow. The vehicle plodded around the circular path of the grounds, and as I passed the cemetery's entrance and slowed down for a look, I noticed an avalanche of snow careening off the plow's left side, making the area where David had spent his final living moments even more ensconced.

The brake lights of the truck flashed red and it moved to the right to make way for David's vehicle, which was pulled to the side of the path so as not to block it. I veered to the side of the road and parked for a few minutes to see if the plowman would exit his vehicle and check on the car. To my surprise, he didn't.

At the moment it was twenty-nine degrees and there were snow flurries scurrying about. A white landscape that was blinding to look at coalesced with a stone-gray sky, and the current light snowfall was doing its part to make driving visibility worse and bury everything deeper yet.

But weather in Illinois and in the Midwest in general can be unpredictable. That evening it warmed up to forty-three degrees. I don't often give the weather much thought, but when I woke up the next morning and headed to work, I was amazed to discover it was a balmy fifty degrees outside and sunny—with the temperature expected to hit an unbelievable fifty-nine degrees by the afternoon. The world around me was thawing out with a vengeance: snow was melting and mushy brown grass was spreading into view; formerly sturdy icicles were dripping water like leaky faucets; dirty water was spewing and splashing from car tires. Given the change in weather, I wasn't surprised the next day when I saw on the *C-U Journal's* website that the body of David Kendrick had been found.

What did surprise me, however, was a story about David's life that I read in the newspaper a few days later.

Chapter 9

David had made his fortune in pharmaceuticals, which I suppose shouldn't have surprised me, given that he had handed me a white pill that was untraceable and killed. He'd graduated with three degrees from the University of Illinois at Chicago, two of them in the field of medicine and one in engineering, and then had worked as a doctor in the Chicago and downstate areas for more than a decade. In his forties, he and a scientist colleague started a pharmaceutical company that performed research and worked to find cures for debilitating diseases such as leukemia, Parkinson's, influenza, and diabetes. David's passion for helping autistic children live easier lives was also mentioned.

I discovered from the article that Jared, David's son, had been autistic and had died under "mysterious circumstances" when he was twenty-seven. Jared had lived with his parents and one morning had not woken up. According to the article, David and Phyllis were both interviewed by authorities about their son's death but not considered suspects.

David's company thrived, but it eventually splintered into two entities. I skimmed this portion of the article, getting lost in the minutia of the rough spots he'd had with his former partner and the dealings that had taken place with each newly formed company.

David was from the Champaign area, not surprising since he'd related the story about the rooftop dancing extravaganza where he'd fallen for his future wife. David and Phyllis had returned downstate from the Chicago suburbs later in life to live a quiet existence in Mahomet. He had served on numerous boards and had contributed to several charities over the years. David, it seemed, had been a well-respected member of the medical community in Illinois.

I wished the piece had said more about the puzzling manner in which Jared had died. Was it inconceivable that David, who years later would ask me to kill his wife because of various illnesses she was suffering through, might have ended his own son's life in a premature fashion? Perhaps the strain of living with an autistic adult had gotten under his skin and he'd wanted to find an easy way out. And maybe Phyllis had suspected something amiss where her only child's death was concerned and had grown to hate her husband because of it.

Furthermore, maybe it was the scrutiny surrounding the cause of his son's death that had forced David to ask someone else to do the dirty work the second time around with his wife—me.

I wanted to tell Emily about all this but didn't yet feel up to the task. And talking to Trevor about David's death wasn't an option, either. In fact, I hoped I was right and Trevor paid little attention to the local news, because if he did find out about David's heart attack, I would have some serious explaining to do.

On Christmas Eve I presented an expensive diamond bracelet to my stunned wife, who was pleased but also concerned about how I was able to afford it. Emily's skeptical look faded after I told her I'd been putting money aside for several years. Even then I don't think she was convinced it was the right purchase to make, but she did rave about the gift.

It was a strange time. My mom was getting worse by the day, dying. We were secret millionaires, but I'd stolen the cash from a man who had died right in front of me. I couldn't begin to fathom how we were going to handle all the money we now had, which was still sitting in the suitcase in a closet upstairs.

I began to lose focus at work, thinking that because I was now a rich man, what difference did it make which vendors got what amount of ad space in our meaningless radio-control catalog? Without Emily's knowledge, I began calling in sick and taking vacation days more than ever before, carrying hundred dollar bills with me as I drove off to nearby towns, spending money in a meandering, pointless fashion.

Not long after Christmas, when I should have been at work but was instead eating lunch and watching TV in a booth at a downtown bar, Chad walked up to me and said hello.

"Mmm, hey, Chad," I uttered, swallowing a fry and then taking a drink of Pepsi. "What are you doing here?"

“I work here. I’m a busboy, cook, bartender—whatever they need, really. What are *you* doing here is the question?”

“Oh, I’m just on my lunch hour.”

He gave me a puzzled look. “Is today extra-casual day or something?”

I looked at him, not sure what he was talking about.

“Your clothes, silly.”

I looked down at my grungy sweatshirt and tattered jeans and felt exposed. Emily had traveled up north to her parents’ place that morning, leaving the house before I did, so I’d skipped work and hadn’t bothered to put on my normal office attire, which I’d been doing sometimes lately to fool her into thinking I was actually going to work. “Some of the office workers help in the warehouse after Christmas, so we have the option to wear jeans.” This was true, but in actuality I’d never once been asked to help in the Hobby Town warehouse.

“Gotcha.” To my dismay, Chad slid into the seat across from me and leaned forward. “Did you hear about that David guy?”

I felt blood rushing to my cheeks but tried to play it cool. “I did, yeah.”

“Isn’t that effed up! In the cemetery where we met him, no less.”

Chad was being too loud, but I didn’t tell him to pipe down. Instead, all I said was, “It was sad.”

“It was also a little *weird*, don’t you think, considering we just met him and what he asked us to do. Who would have thought *he* would go first, before his wife.”

“How’d you hear about it?”

“A friend of mine who I work with here told me about it. It was all over the news.”

“Yeah, it was.”

“Anyway, I don’t really see your brother as much anymore, so I haven’t had a chance to tell him. Does he know?”

“Yeah, I mentioned it to him. He thought it was crazy too.”

Chad asked about my mom’s health and if I had any plans for New Year’s Eve. My answers were distracted and vague. Instead of just saying no about New Year's Eve, I rambled on about possible plans that Emily and I might have, all the while reconciling in my head that Trevor would now have to learn about David's death, and that Chad's knowing about it could perhaps be detrimental to our cause, though I couldn't yet formulate in my mind how. Angry at myself for wandering around town with no real purpose, I made a vow that this would be the last time I ran into Chad in such a careless way.

Ignoring my advice to not contact each other by phone, Trevor called me at nine p.m. from a downtown bar on New Year's Eve, sounding in good spirits. He was out with Chad and they wanted me to join them. I told him I'd think about it.

"You should go," Emily said. "You've been under so much stress and sadness with your mom lately. Go let off some steam with your brother. You guys are bonding more these days anyway. Remember how fun it was when he came over for dinner?"

"But New Year's Eve?" I whined. "Of all nights to go out."

"Oh, you *never* go out. You should do it. I'll give you a ride there."

"Do you want to come?"

"No, not really. Just go out and have fun. Most guys would kill to have their wives give them that order."

I started to waver, thinking it might be nice to have some drinks but not wild about seeing my brother or Chad.

Emily kept pushing. "Take a cab home if you drink too much, and don't let them get you too drunk. They're younger, you know."

So I showered and dragged myself out to 10 Deep, a trendy nightclub I'd been to a few times before with Emily and loathed. The place was packed, and at first I wondered if I even had the "credentials" to get in—a tough-looking bouncer was sizing people up in a scrutinizing fashion that I found menacing.

But I did get in, and right away I saw that Trevor and Chad had seats at the bar. I joined them and stood by their stools as revelers tried to slither through the area to place drink orders.

"Look what the cat dragged in!" Chad shouted. He pecked me on the cheek, a drunken act I didn't expect. Trevor shook my hand, barely looking at me. Chad ordered me a mixed drink without asking what I wanted. I turned to look at the amped-up crowd.

There were couches with coffee tables along the side where groups of people lounged. Stuffed chairs were spread throughout, giving the atmosphere a hint of casualness. Most people were standing or milling about; some were headed toward the back where the VIP balcony and dance floor awaited. Four bartenders were racing around behind the gold and glittery bar counter, two men and two women, all four of them young, beautiful people who were under a great deal of stress at the moment.

The place was full: singles, couples, friends, university students, probably some townies, and people ages thirty and over like me. Several work colleagues came up to greet me, and all at once I was whisked away to the darkened dance area in back, where bodies

crushed against one another and an AC/DC song, mixed with a loud techno beat, blasted from the speakers. I was handed a shot and asked to contribute to a group toast in honor of the coming year. In jest and on the spot, I toasted to world peace and a Final Four appearance by the University of Illinois basketball team. But as I choked down the burning clear liquor, whatever it was, I offered up a silent wish that no trouble would stem from my involvement with David.

New drinks were placed in my hand like clockwork, and at some fuzzy point, not a care in the world, I was dancing to loud, thumping house music. It was fun. One guy from the marketing team shouted in my ear that he'd "never seen me drunk and kickin' it before." Another coworker, a brunette who worked the phones in the sales department and who I didn't really know, grabbed my hand and pulled me close to dance with her. This went on for several songs that melded together, and then, all at once, I began to feel claustrophobic and guilty, wondering what my brother and Chad were doing, wishing Emily had come out with me.

Standing on my tiptoes, I peered outward from the center of the dance floor, locking eyes with Chad right away. He waved me over and I left the packed group of dancers without a word.

"Your bro is in the bathroom!" Chad yelled above the din. "Let's scoot over to Chintzy's Haven across the street. We can get good martinis and it'll be much quieter. I'm bored with this joint."

The booze had made me relaxed and confident. I was emboldened and ready to plunge into the cold night air and strut across the street; prepared to discuss anything about the money with Trevor and Chad, whatever thoughts and questions might be chucked my way.

"Oh, and by the way," Chad added, "we'll put the drinks on *your* tab since you can no doubt more than afford it."

And on my tab the drinks went—many drinks. In the midst of

like-minded celebrators, we openly talked about the money at our table while drinking gargantuan amounts of alcohol.

Chintzy's Haven was a long, modish bar with numerous tables lining both sides, lots of modern artwork, and three stairs that led down to a wider space where large, comfy chairs were scattered throughout. Like 10 Deep it had a cosmopolitan look and vibe, which I knew Trevor and Chad dug.

We sat down, and Chad started right in on me. "So imagine our surprise," he began, in a dramatic voice, "when I mentioned to Trevor here that David died, and lo and behold, he tells me he didn't know about that fact and had never heard anything about it from you."

I stared at my drink, saying nothing.

"Why'd you lie?" Chad demanded. "You told me that you told Trevor about David dying—*so* not true at all. And how, exactly, did you get the money? Trevor told me you had it. Tell us everything and no fibbing and no leaving anything out."

I swallowed and cleared my throat, pretending to be humbled

by Chad's rebuke. "Remember when we were leaving the cemetery that last time and I got out of the car to talk to David?"

Chad nodded and Trevor avoided my eyes.

"Well, that's when I decided to agree to do what he wanted done. To his wife."

"So you lied to us when you got back in the car?" Chad asked.

"Yes."

"And?" Chad prodded.

"And ... I went out there again to meet him like he and I planned ... and I assume you know about the rest since you know he died. The guy had a heart attack right in front of me. So I took his money and got the fuck out of there."

They each gawked at me, surprised looks plastered on their faces, along with, I would have sworn to it, a hint of admiration.

"Where's the money now?" Chad inquired.

"It's safe."

"Is it at your house?"

"It's hidden and it's safe, Chad."

He pulled out a cigarette from his pack and shook his head in dismay. "This isn't right. *We*, me and Trevor, deserve a share of that money as much as you. David himself said we would get a split of it."

"David's dead now," I said.

"So what, nothing changes regarding who gets the money. You didn't do anything to earn it more than we did."

"The hell I didn't," I retorted. "I made the trip out to the cemetery and I got it free and clear."

Trevor shook his head in disgust. "You told me you didn't want me going with you that night. I wish I had now."

"Yeah, and you went out there without me knowing anything about it at *all*," Chad said. "If you had done what David wanted with his wife, then I could see why you would deserve a bigger piece of the pie—but you didn't do anything. We should each get a third of the cash and call it a day."

"Chad, we'll split it up and call it a day when I'm ready to do that," I said.

A threatening edge must have come through in my words, because Chad's demeanor and tone seemed more respectful when he asked his next question.

"Can you at least give me a few thousand bones, like you did with Trevor?"

"Maybe."

Chad leaned in close to me. "I think you can do better than 'maybe.' After all, you own a little secret about David Kendrick that the cops would just be *dying* to know."

"What? That he had a heart attack?"

"That and the small fact that you stole five million of his dollars. That money isn't rightfully yours, Alex."

"If you go to the cops you'll ruin it for all of us. I might get in trouble for stealing, but if you rat me out, Chad, none of us will get anything. Is that what you want?"

"No."

I laughed. "You two wouldn't last ten minutes in prison."

The statement seemed to take them aback. "Why, because

we're gay?" Chad asked. "Something tells me you wouldn't last too long in prison either, pretty boy. And let me just say, you'd be there *much* longer than the both of us for taking that money. Trevor and I didn't even do anything wrong, when you get down to it."

"Bullshit," I countered. "You sat there and listened to David talk about having us kill his wife. I didn't see you reporting that information to the authorities."

"Okay, okay," Trevor interjected. "Let's quit talking about all this stuff and just have some fun. It's New Year's Eve! Why in the world are we even talking about jail? Let's just let David's death blow over and wait a few months. After that, we can divvy up the loot and go our separate ways."

"A few *months*!" Chad exclaimed.

"What do you mean, 'go our separate ways'? Where are you going to go?" I asked Trevor.

"I don't know. Anywhere but here."

"I'm out of here too," Chad said.

The idea of Trevor leaving Champaign, the only place he'd ever known, and moving on to a new life and probably losing touch with me altogether—it made me feel dejected.

"What are you guys going to do with your share?" Chad asked, sounding like an excited five-year-old kid.

What followed was a predictable litany of all the glamorous things the three of us intended to do with our newfound fortunes. Though I got into the spirit of the conversation despite myself, what I wanted to tell them was that, though investing and saving would help, one point seven million dollars was not going to stretch out in our lifetimes like it might have twenty, thirty, or fifty years ago.

Two point five million, or five million, for that matter, was much more to my liking.

It didn't shock me that Trevor had leaked to Chad that I was holding the cash, but I was still disappointed in him. As I listened to the two of them gab about the money and other straying subjects, I was concocting ways we could eliminate Chad from the picture. Maybe it was the alcohol's encouraging influence, but I thought I had a pretty creative way to do it.

I opened my eyes and saw Emily.

"Welcome back," she said.

"Mmmmm," I moaned, my head throbbing in pain.

"You guys were *so* obnoxious last night," Emily said, as if relating this information right away was imperative.

"What time is it?"

"Almost eleven."

I massaged my forehead, trying to piece together what had happened toward the end of the night. The three of us had piled into a cab, welcoming in the New Year at a third bar—this one not as fashionable as the previous two—where I saw yet more rowdy friends and acquaintances living it up. Plastic hats and champagne had been passed out just before the clock ticked to midnight, and more dancing had occurred even though it wasn't a dance bar per se. After that we'd stopped at an all-night diner where half the city seemed to be. Then at last home via a cab, all of it a hazy blur.

"I don't know why they had to stay the night here, Alex. You and that Chad guy were fighting. And you weren't making any sense. Trevor was trying to calm you both down and you tried to hit him."

"I tried to hit Trevor? What? I don't remember any fighting."

"Well, there was plenty of it. Did you make a bet with him or something?"

"Who? Chad?"

"Yeah."

"No."

"Well, there was a lot of talk about money."

This got my attention. "Um, well, we did argue about who was going to pick up the tab at the bar we were at. It was quite a bit." I waited for her to speak, hoping my response would be satisfactory.

"Geez, Alex, I didn't think you'd get so drunk. Your mom

called this morning. She's really tired, but she wants us to come over later and have dinner."

Thinking about my mom made me feel even more down. "What'd you tell her?"

"I said I'd go and that I wasn't sure about you since you were doing some stuff around the house. Do you want to go?"

"Yeah," I said in a soft voice. "Did you tell her Trevor and I went out last night?"

"No."

"Good. What time are we going over there?"

"I told her around five. Is that okay?"

"Yeah. Where's Trevor?"

"He and Chad were leaving right when I got back from the grocery store earlier. They barely said hello to me. Your brother's always sneaking off in the morning, isn't he?"

To my surprise, Trevor joined us at our parents' house. I hid my hungover state from Mom and Dad as best I could, but Trevor's grumpiness gave him away. While Dad watched football on TV and Emily and Mom stole off to the sunroom to chat, Trevor and I snuck off to the den and tried to decipher what had happened the previous night.

"What were Chad and I fighting about when we got home?" I asked. Trevor was slumped in my dad's desk chair, his long, skinny legs stretched out before him. I was sprawled out on the short white couch.

"You were making crazy, expensive bets about all these fucked-up things and then trying to act all tough about what you were betting about. It was ridiculous. And then you started in on me, trying to punch me when I tried to calm you guys both down."

"Yeah, Emily told me about that. I'm sorry."

I saw the corner of Trevor's lip go upward, I guess indicating he halfway accepted my apology. "Hey, I'm afraid to ask, but did we bring up the money in front of Emily?"

"I don't think so, but she was looking at you guys like you

had both lost your minds."

It hurt me to hear that. I had always made it a point to never get out of control around Emily, and a night of hard drinking had botched that. Emily had been acting reserved around me all day, and I could sense her disappointment in me. I wondered if I'd perhaps let something slip last night that perplexed her, something about the money.

"Well, on another note, I'd like to say congratulations, Trevor. You've cost us both about a million dollars each by telling Chad about the cash I had."

He sat there for a moment, looking stung, and then, in a defiant tone, said, "Get off your high horse, Alex. We don't need it all for ourselves. Chad's right. We were both there too when we first met David, so Chad *is* part of it. Remember what I said in the beginning? We're a team through all of this."

I wanted to tell him off and say about four things in rebuttal, but Trevor, perhaps sensing my slow-witted state of mind, cut me short by bringing up something else altogether.

“I was listening to Janis Joplin this morning when I got home,” he said. “Sometimes I listen to her music when I’m hungover and feeling bad about myself. Do you like Janis Joplin?”

I shrugged, staring at the threadbare soles of his argyle socks.

“I love her.” Trevor cleared his throat and said, “I know you probably don’t want to hear this, but she was someone who helped give me the confidence to come out when I was still in high school.”

I nodded my head, giving Trevor only the slightest indication that I cared.

“It was the song ‘Maybe’ on the radio. She was singing it live, and it nearly brought me to tears, Alex, I’m not kidding. I was driving home from school, a little pissed off at some things that were happening, and I hear this confident, soulful, *bluesy* woman on the radio just belting out these words that came from the heart like nobody’s business.”

I nodded. Janis Joplin, from what I knew of her at Woodstock or some hippy place like that, did have a set of pipes.

"And she's just singing in this heartfelt way that made me ache, and yet ... it made me happy. I felt deep down this woman seemed to be in as much pain as I was, yet she was using her considerable talent to throw it all to the wind and just go forward. It was beautiful. I actually had to stop driving and pull over until the end of the song."

"Wow. So you came out right after you heard the song?"

"Well, it didn't happen just like that, but yes. I mean, yes, after hearing Janis and going home and doing some soul searching, yes, it wasn't long after that that I made myself become more ... unafraid, you know? I became who I wanted to be and said to hell with everyone else. Because really, for maybe the first time in my life, even though I had friends to share my anxieties with, I'd never taken it beyond that. Janis showed me, through that one song, that there was a whole other world of weirdos out there like me, searching for themselves and the realness in others."

"Cool."

"You don't care, do you?"

"I don't know, Trevor. I've got other things on my mind besides Janis Joplin. Didn't she die when she was like twenty-three or something?"

"Twenty-seven."

I sat there looking at the wall in front of me, unable to muster any sentimental feelings toward Trevor. So the hell what if he had come out of his self-absorbed closet with the voice of Janis Joplin urging him on. What mattered to me was the future, not Trevor's hungover wistfulness over a long-dead musical artist.

"We really need to decide what we're going to do," I said. "It's time to make some hard decisions."

Just then I heard footsteps coming down the hall—Emily's.

"What's going on, guys?" She sauntered into the room holding a coffee mug and blowing on it, sexy in her tight blue jeans and a tight brown sweater. I'd wanted her all day but had gotten the brush-off.

“We’re just talking,” I said.

“You guys are inseparable these days,” she said.

Trevor and I looked at one another.

“I wouldn’t go that far,” I said.

Emily was looking around the room, taking in the décor. “Why don’t you come in and talk to your mom and me instead of hiding out back here? I won’t tell her you’re both hungover, but I think she suspects something is up.”

She laughed at this statement as we pulled ourselves up to follow her out of the room—both of us with a little reluctance, I think—leaving the matter of the money shelved for another day.

Chapter 10

A new year had arrived, so I decided to get my act together. I threw myself into my job, no longer skipping work on a whim, but instead working through lunch on some days and staying in the office after regular work hours on a steady basis. Far from behaving like a bigshot millionaire with plenty of money stowed away, I lived and spent in a frugal manner, disregarding the stash in the closet as if it were nonexistent. And when the thought of the large suitcase did pop into my head, it conjured a surprising emotion: annoyance. It was a startling thing, given my former obsession with the money and the possibilities it offered.

Out of nowhere, my mom started gaining strength and improving, giving our family hope.

Then Emily announced to me one night she was pregnant. She'd taken two home pregnancy tests and visited the doctor. This news changed our world, and Emily and I began talking about the future in earnest, excited that there would be a new member of our family. She'd never been more joyful.

By the end of January, I began to forget about the money entirely. The hidden cash was a reassurance—there if we needed it, yes, but not a necessity.

One Saturday during the late afternoon, while I was at home working on the computer and Emily was out shopping, Trevor stopped by our house. He'd gotten his license back and bought a car—an old beater that a friend had sold to him for almost nothing—and was driving again after a long absence from the road. I knew something was wrong the second he walked in the door. His eyes had red rings around them, like he'd been crying on the way over or was up too late last night doing drugs or was sick with worry. Maybe, I thought with a sense of dread, it was all of these things.

"Sorry to bother you," he mumbled, looking down at the floor. His thick hair was unruly and getting longer, giving him a frazzled, scuzzy look.

"Come in, you're not bothering me. Do you want some

coffee? There's some left over from this morning."

"That'd be great," he croaked. "Why are you wearing khakis and a sweater? Are you going somewhere?"

We moved into the kitchen. "No, just hanging out. Hey, guess what, Trevor?"

"What?"

"Emily's pregnant."

His eyes lit up. "Oh, Alex, that's wonderful. I'm so happy for you both." It looked like he was thinking about hugging me but didn't. "Do you know the gender yet?"

"No, it's too early. We're thinking of names right now for either a boy or a girl."

"That's such great news."

I put down the two empty coffee cups I was holding and walked over to where he was sitting, placing a hand on his shoulder. "Trevor, what's wrong?"

"I don't mean to spoil your news, Alex. I'm sorry. It's just … it's Chad."

I took my hand off of him and walked back to the coffee pot, saying nothing, waiting for him to proceed. "What about Chad?" I finally asked, pouring us each a cup of coffee.

"He broke up with me. For good. He wants to leave here, go somewhere warm to live, and he doesn't want to take me with."

As I headed toward the microwave, I could see Trevor's hurt was genuine. I punched in the time and hit the "Start" button. The inside of the microwave lit up and the two cups spun slowly around like a hesitant merry-go-round. "You could do so much better than Chad," I told him, not turning around. "I thought you said you didn't want to be with him long-term anyway."

"Well, maybe I didn't know what I was talking about. You don't know him as well as I do."

I removed the heated cups and walked back over to him. "Trevor," I said, reaching out to give his shoulder a shake, "really, you could do much better. He's not even that nice of a guy, is he? He seems like a goof to me."

He looked away, and at first I thought he wasn't going to say much more. Then, like a waterfall, the words sprang forth.

"Chad and I met at a wedding three years ago."

"Yeah. And?"

Trevor sighed as he massaged his temples. "Do you mind indulging me? I just need someone to talk to."

"Sure. Go on."

"So this wedding we met at, we were the only gay guys there, and we clicked instantly. In a half hour's time, I was telling him things about myself that I only reserve for people I'm close to. He was easy to talk to and very nice, despite what *you* might think.

"And he opened up to *me*, too," Trevor went on. "He loved music, movies, actors and actresses from different decades. I never knew much about pop culture until I met Chad."

I smiled. "You know your stuff now, that's for sure." Trevor's overflow of knowledge about the world of entertainment never failed to amaze my parents and me.

"Yeah, that's thanks to Chad. Anyway, I thought I had a

winner on the car ride home from the wedding. I didn't have a car, and he had a really cool one that he later sold, unfortunately, so he gave me a lift. And while we were driving home, the song 'Girls Just Want to Have Fun' by Cindy Lauper came on. You've heard it, right?"

"Of course."

"We sang along with it, happy as all get-out, and when it was over, he turned down the volume and told me that the chorus of the song might have felt joyous but is actually very dispiriting."

"Really? Why?"

"He said that years and years of women being persecuted and subjugated all over the world could be heard in Cindy Lauper's tone."

"Okay."

"Listen to the song sometime, Alex. Listen to her voice outside the realm of what you may think she's trying to convey—you know, some party girl just looking for a good time. Her voice sounds longing in the chorus, not at all that independent and happy. It's almost like she's asking permission from the world to let girls have fun and expecting a negative response. It's like she knows she's going to be refused, but she's giving it her all to find out if freedom is possible. If you listen closely, it's like she wants to be liberated but knows it's never going to happen.

"And actually, I found out not too long ago that Cindy Lauper *was* sheltered and restricted by her managers and entourage during her heyday in the eighties because they didn't trust her to just go out and be herself while she was out on tour. So it turns out Chad was right about what he was hearing."

"That's interesting. Here, drink your coffee," I said, scooting the warm cup closer to him. "I'll have to listen to the song more carefully next time."

"He really does come up with all this poignant stuff that you may not think he has in him. Some people think he's narcissistic, but he's actually not at all. He's opened up so many avenues for me in terms of the way I think. He doesn't blindly follow what everybody considers to be normal, and I've always liked that about him."

"Yeah, there's something to be said for that." I sprinkled sugar and then poured cream into my coffee, watching the dark liquid cloud up. I slid both containers to Trevor. "So where does he want to go?"

"He talks mostly about California."

"Do you want to go out there?"

"With the right person. Chad."

" Come on. Would you *really* want to follow him out to California?"

"Well, not now, of course. Not *follow* him. But if he loved me ..."

"But it sounds like he doesn't love you."

"I know that, Alex."

"And he ... when it comes to the money—not to change the subject—he seems to have no regard for all the danger it represents."

Trevor thought about this. “I don’t know. Sometimes I think you worry too much about—”

“On New Year’s Eve, when we all went out together—”

“And you guys were complete idiots.”

I chuckled. “Yeah, the night we were complete idiots, he definitely was asking for his share of the money that night. And he wanted to cut you out of getting any. He mentioned dividing it up between just him and me,” I lied.

“What?”

“I mean, at least that’s what he said late into the night, when he was wasted. He probably doesn’t even remember saying it now.”

“What exactly did he say?” Trevor asked, looking confused.

“It just seemed like he felt that cutting you out of your share would be an easy thing to do. That’s mostly how I remember it, anyway, and it made me mad.”

“How ... I mean, why? Why do you think he thought that? Or did he say?”

"I just think he views you as a bit of a doormat, someone who isn't willing to fight for what's his; that you maybe have an easy come, easy go type of mentality that's easy to take advantage of. It was my impression that he thought we could leave you out and that it wouldn't be hard to do."

Trevor nodded. His face was somber. "I don't believe you, Alex."

"Well, believe it or don't, Trevor, I don't really care." I stood up and walked to the sink, looking out the window. A squirrel was nibbling on bird food that had spilled from our bird feeder. "Like I said, he was loaded when he told me this. He's never brought it up again, and he probably doesn't even remember saying it."

"Ooh, this sounds like something scandalous," Emily said in a playful voice. "Who was loaded and doesn't remember saying something?"

I jumped. "Geez, Emily! Don't sneak up on us like that."

She was holding some shopping bags. "So sorry to interrupt,

Alex. I thought you heard me come in."

"It's okay. You just surprised the hell out of me. I didn't hear you at all."

"The front door was cracked open. One of you must have left it like that."

"It was me," Trevor said. "Sorry, Em."

"No, it's okay," she responded, giving Trevor a quick hug. "Are you guys okay? I now feel like I interrupted something."

"We're fine," I said. "I'm just used to you coming in through the garage."

"I parked in the driveway because I might run out again."

"Gotcha."

"Okay, well, I'm going to run this stuff upstairs," she said, holding the bags up higher for me to see. "Don't worry, it's not as bad as it looks. Mostly clearance items from Bergner's. See you later, Trevor."

We both waited for her to leave the room and head upstairs. "I'm so sick of keeping all this stuff about the money from her,"

I admitted to Trevor.

"Just tell her already. She's your wife. She'll understand about the circumstances … or most of them, anyway. She has to know eventually, right?"

"I guess so, yeah."

"Alex, I think it's time we just split up the money between the three of us—you, me, and Chad—and be done with it."

"We've been through this before, Trevor. Chad's not getting any money, and that's how it's going to be."

"But it *is* also Chad's money, if we have any kind of a conscience. And I'm saying this as someone who's no longer with him. I've been thinking about it, and it's ridiculous that that money is just sitting here in your house, not being used by anybody. That makes no sense. It's not just yours, Alex. It's time to split it up and part ways. The three of us found out about it together, so the three of us should all get it—evenly and fair and square."

"Trevor, you're right that it's time to make some decisions, but I'm not backing down about Chad. He's too much of a liability with all that cash."

"I don't think he'd be as careless with it as you think."

"Do you want to hear my idea?"

"What idea?"

"Can I come over to your apartment tonight to talk?"

"I guess so."

"How does seven sound?"

"That's fine. Do you want to tell me what you have in mind right now, give me the abridged version?"

"No, not now. I feel bad and need to make peace with Emily. She's mad at me."

Trevor smiled for the first time since walking in the house. "Yeah, you were a bit paranoid with her just now."

She was lying on her left side reading a book. Her body had a tautness to it, which told me she wanted to be left alone. A singular circle of light from the lamp on the bedside table was shining outward, enveloping Emily's head and upper body in the room's only illumination, save for the opened blinds that allowed in the day's gloom.

"What are you reading?" I asked in a gentle voice.

"A novel. Just started it."

"Is it any good?"

"It's okay so far. Your mom loaned it to me."

"What's it about?"

"A husband who is mean to his wife and shuts her out."

"Mean to his wife?" I snaked my way onto the bed to get close and placed my hand on her rump, rubbing. "Is that what you think I am? Mean."

"You were downstairs."

"I know. I'm sorry."

She turned to face me. "What's going on with you and Trevor? You guys are thick as thieves lately. Are you talking about your mom and her cancer?"

"No, it's not that. His boyfriend broke up with him, so he was feeling down and wanted to come over and talk. I was just as surprised as you that he came over."

"Who said I was surprised that he came over, Alex? I wasn't at all surprised he was here. Not these days."

I turned to lie on my back, pulling my arms up and locking my hands behind my head as if I were contemplating the mysteries of life on our plain white ceiling.

"I'm not trying to pry," Emily continued. "I think it's great that Trevor is confiding in you about personal stuff. I want you guys to be close, of course. But the way you were acting when I surprised you just now—and even that time at your parents' house on New Year's Day, now that I think about it—I feel like you're hiding something."

"When it comes to Trevor, Emily, I just don't always know what to ... how to talk to him or help him the way he wants. Our lives are so different. *We're* very different. So we were talking about what was going on with him and some stuff about his personal life, and then you walked in and it just surprised me is all."

I paused for a moment before going on. "And there's also this element of, you know, when I bring this stuff up to you, I think of your family and how perfect it is, and how mine is so screwed up."

There. I had communicated enough generalities to answer her but also convoluted things so that nothing of substance had really been said.

"Oh, Alex, we've been through this a million times. My family is *not* perfect. No family is. And your family, by the way, is not as screwed up as you always say it is."

"Maybe not. But you have to admit we've got our share of issues. Trevor is just ... well, he's become a new person to me again, and I'm just trying to help him through some stuff, some of which includes issues with my mom being sick. But I really am sorry about freaking out downstairs, especially in front of Trevor."

"I don't care that it was in front of Trevor," she said, shifting her left leg on top of me and laying her arm across my chest. "I just want you to love me."

We fell asleep like that for an hour or so and made love after we awoke.

Afterward, as Emily slept, I thought back to a blustery Easter Sunday when I was visiting home from college and Trevor was a teenager. We were having a family reunion at Lake Mahomet and my brother was flying a new kite that had been given to him earlier that day by our grandparents. Trevor used to love kites and had collected them. The flying wasn't going so well due to fading winds, and at some point, having given up on making the kite airborne, Trevor headed toward where I was sitting in a grassy area near the beach, where lots of chairs were spread about. To this day I'm not sure if Trevor knew I was there, observing three thuggish-looking kids striding his way, enclosing him all at once. Their body language bespoke bullishness, a chance to pounce on my flouncy brother, perhaps razz him about his appearance or his kite. A kid stepped up to snatch the kite, breaking it in two, and I did nothing but sit there, watching, waiting, *hoping* these guys would push the envelope a bit more, put a real scare into my brother, who was staving off tears. Not much more happened, but it never fails to hit me, every time I think about this distant memory, how casual I was about the whole incident.

How I had wanted something bad to happen to my brother.

I went back to sleep. When I woke up, I focused my bleary eyes onto the red digits of the clock radio. It was eight o'clock, an hour past my designated meeting time with Trevor. Startled at just how out of it I was, I roused myself up and told Emily to stay in bed.

"I have to run out real quick, but I'll bring home some pizza," I said, giving her a lightning-fast kiss. "We'll have a very late dinner."

"Where are you going?" Emily murmured, as I left the room.

Trevor was startled by my proposal, but I was tired of putting things off. It was time to *act* if we wanted to keep the money in the family, a fact I kept repeating to him. After a while, the safe feeling that Chad would not be hanging over us like a bad omen for the rest of our lives—if we took the appropriate action—appealed to Trevor. It took some convincing, though, some reassurances that I would take the brunt of any bad aftershocks of our scheme—and even then it was no sure bet that trouble wouldn't land on him. Trevor knew this. He wasn't stupid.

Emily was awake downstairs when I got home much later than I'd intended. The pizza place had been packed and I'd been stuck waiting in line for an inordinate amount of time. Content to be together, we stuffed our faces with pizza and watched a nostalgic movie from the eighties.

Chapter 11

I picked up the guys at eight-fifteen p.m. in the parking lot of the downtown train station. It was a good meeting place since both of their apartments were nearby. Trevor had contacted Chad earlier in the week and cajoled him into coming to my house for drinks and then a night out on the town. We also promised to give him his share of the loot, which sealed the deal.

If Trevor felt uncomfortable because of his relationship status with Chad, he didn't show it during the car ride to my house. From the moment he stepped into the car, Trevor had a glow about him and a beaming, satiated presence, which seemed to have a positive effect on Chad, who was likewise jovial. We pulled into my driveway and I parked in the garage, right away shutting the garage door and hopping out of the car.

"In the spirit of the occasion—Chad's going-away party—I've got plenty of booze, some games we can play, and lots of CDs," I announced. "I'm also our designated driver for the evening, when we go out later, so live it up, guys."

Chad patted me on the back on the way inside. "I'm *lovin'* this guy!" he gushed.

Both of them ogled the many bottles and cans sitting on the kitchen counter, some of which had been in our cabinet for ages. I doled out the assignments straightaway: "Trevor, you're the bartender for the evening. Chad, can you handle music duties?"

"Sure," he responded, at once walking to the stereo in the family room. "Bartender, make me a Beam and Diet, will ya?"

"Coming up," Trevor answered.

"Where did your wife go?" Chad yelled from the family room.

"She's at her parent's house up near Chicago!" I yelled back. "She goes there about once every two or three months, and I imagine that'll increase once the baby is born."

"Oh yeah, you're gonna be a dad!" Chad shouted above the din of the music he'd selected. "Congratulations!"

"Thank you!"

Chad had put on a Who CD and was singing the chorus to "I

Can See for Miles." Trevor had made us all drinks. After some chitchat, we started a game of spades in the kitchen. It was hard to ignore Chad's irritable habit of thumping down his cards in time with the beat of the music, their edges clicking as they struck the kitchen counter. He was drinking fast, laughing with gusto, and in a swaggering mood, which seemed to subdue Trevor's temperament.

Halfway through the second game, Chad abruptly threw down his cards and said, "When I'm all settled in out in Cali, you guys are more than welcome to come visit. Anytime, Alex, my buddy. And you know you can bring your wife, right?"

"Cool, thank you," I replied, taking a sip of the drink Trevor had concocted for me. "Emily would love to go out there. I would too."

Chad turned to Trevor. "And when you find a man who's ten times better than me, you guys can come out and we'll all go clubbing. The scene is pretty fierce out there."

I couldn't tell if Trevor was saddened or repulsed by the offer;

maybe both emotions surfaced. Either way, he had a look on his face that was hard to measure, and I think Chad noticed, too. He clapped Trevor on the back and jumped up to change the music. "Mix me a White Russian," he ordered.

By ten thirty I was ready to go, but it was hard to get a word in edgewise. Chad and Trevor were red-faced and drunk, arguing about whatever pop-culture topic came to the forefront. Chad took to heart his role as DJ and slid in a new CD every two or three minutes, not even letting entire songs play through. He talked about the legend behind every artist he played, relating stuff I couldn't have cared less about. His inside knowledge captivated Trevor, though, so I feigned interest. According to Chad, Def Leppard's drummer, Rick Allen, kept his severed left arm floating in formaldehyde in a tightly sealed glass case that hung on his living room wall for all to see within his beautiful Malibu home. Such topics came and went.

When the entertainment-related discussions fizzled out, Chad and Trevor couldn't stop reminiscing about their relationship, both the good and bad. Spontaneous hugs were exchanged, as were dramatic promises to never lose touch, to always remain close friends. Once I even noticed Trevor veering toward tears, but Chad had a knack for lightening the mood with the ease of any good charmer, and in no time they became nostalgic again, laughing with unbridled glee.

It was a strange thing, hearing and watching my brother act in such an open manner with his ex-boyfriend. I was glad when he got up to go to the bathroom—the momentary silence from all their talking was a welcome relief.

"Have you ever been out to Cameron Park, Chad?" I asked.

He took a drink and made a thoughtful face. "I don't think so. Is it in Savoy?"

"No, it's out on Staley Road. It's fairly new."

"Staley Road. I remember *that* night."

It took me a second to realize what Chad was talking about, and then it hit me. "Oh, yeah, the car," I said, remembering the night my otherwise trusty vehicle had died where Staley Road and U.S. 150 intersected. "That was crazy. But anyway, I was thinking we could check out the park before we head out to the bars."

"Um ... you want to visit a closed park before going out?" Chad asked, snickering. "What are we, in high school?"

I humored him with a hearty laugh. "Well, I was thinking we could stop by there for just a few minutes, before we head out for the real fun. I want to get a picture of the three of us, and I thought that would be a cool place to do it."

"A picture?"

"Yeah. On top of this playground structure at Cameron."

"I guess so. It's cold out, but if you really want to."

"Think of the coolest, most high-up jungle gym you've ever seen in your life," said Trevor, who had just returned from the bathroom. "You know, like the ones in parks for little kids."

"Okay," Chad said.

"This is like that but ten times more amazing."

"Sounds cool."

"And I want all three of us to climb to the top to get a picture," I told Chad. "I know it sounds corny, but there's something about the view and overall vibe up there that's special, especially at night. I think you'll like it. Emily and I have taken photos up there before."

"How high up is it?" Chad asked.

"It's not the St. Louis Arch or anything, but it's gotta be ... what, Trevor?"

"Probably forty or fifty feet high."

"Yeah, that sounds about right," I said.

"Well, it sounds pretty cool," Chad said. "I'll go there if you guys want."

"Great! So we'll take a few pictures for posterity, and then it's off to the bars," I said.

"Don't forget about the money," Trevor added.

I nodded my head. "Yep, I know. When we come back here tonight, Chad, after the bars, I'll give you your share in a suitcase and then take you home. Or you can stay the night here, whatever you want to do. Sound good?"

"Sounds great! You're the best, Alex. I can't believe it's finally happening! I love you guys. Drinks are on *me* tonight, okay? How 'bout it?"

"I won't argue with that," Trevor said.

I asked Trevor to collect some bottles of booze and beer and put them in a grocery bag so we could take them with us to the park. Both Trevor and Chad loved this idea.

As we pulled out of the driveway, I don't think either of them noticed that I'd kept all the downstairs lights turned on, leaving part of the house lit up like a Christmas tree, as bright as if I were sitting at home watching TV.

I'd read in the newspaper about Deke Cameron, the local eccentric who had used part of his riches to construct fantastical Cameron Park on the outskirts of Champaign. The property mogul envisioned, invented, and put into existence a Michael Jackson-like playground that catered to kids and adults alike, a place where adults who had retained even a spark of their childlike youth could climb solo or with their kids upon the mighty construction he'd fought tooth and nail with city officials to have built. The fight had been worth it, too. Kids, adults, people in wheelchairs—everybody in town loved Cameron Park.

In the black of night, Cameron's wooden structure had a looming, almost menacing effect. Its sharp angles and spiraling, upward shape reminded me of a medieval castle, something impossible to penetrate—and a structure that oozed with mysteriousness if you did happen to sneak inside.

The pebbles surrounding the structure crunched under our feet as we walked toward it, creating what I felt was a loud, conspicuous sound. I scanned the area and again saw that it was desolate, not a soul anywhere. Looking backward, I noticed the indentations in the rocks where our footsteps had been. Snow was packed in an intermittent fashion against and on top of the wooden walling surrounding the gravel. I looked up and saw only darkness, no stars or moon in sight.

"This is it," I announced to Chad, looking to my right to observe his reaction.

"It is big," he responded, taking a swig of Peach Schnapps.

"Let's go up!" Trevor shouted, running toward the steps that led to the first level. He too held a bottle of something. Chad and I looked at one another, smiled, and then hightailed after him.

The leisurely manner in which one could stroll to the top appealed to me. Yes, there were more daring and intricate ways to climb to the structure's apex, but most preferred the spacious planks that wound around, snake-like, until the highest level was reached.

Trevor pounded upward ahead of us. "Come on, losers! Where you guys at?"

Chad and I huffed and puffed our way upward, trailing him as if we were the lesser contestants in a reality-show competition.

When we reached the pinnacle, there was heavy breathing all around; I saw puffs of air escape everybody's lungs. Chad put down his bottle and rubbed his hands together, spitting off the ledge. The top of the structure reminded me of a pier you might see jutting outward into an ocean. It was around thirty-five feet in length and had the width to accommodate four promenading adults. Trevor surprised me by climbing atop one of the railings and walking on it like a tightrope.

"Geez!" Chad shouted. "Get the hell down from there!"

Trevor jumped back onto the walkway at once, giggling. "Sorry, man."

I pulled out my digital camera. "Chad," I said, startling him. "Take a picture of me and Trevor."

I turned on the camera and handed it over. Trevor and I sat on top of the ledge. If someone had been approaching the playground from the front, he would have seen us sitting on the ledge with our backs to him, arms around one another, smiling for the camera that Chad held. The approaching figure likely would have seen the camera's brief but vivid flash, momentarily brightening the playground's peak with a synthetic burst of light that disappeared after a few seconds.

“Take another,” I said to Chad. This time I gave my brother bunny ears as he sported the peace sign.

“Dorks,” Chad said, as he held down the button and unloaded the second blip of energy from the camera’s white-lighting flash.

“Get in here, Chad,” I said, motioning him over with my right arm and snatching the camera from him. With me in the middle, we all leaned our heads close together as I held the camera outward, hoping for the best. “Smile, guys, we’re rich,” I told them, snapping off the third picture.

They had both laughed at what I’d said before taking the photo, and the result was, I had to admit, a good image when we looked at it moments later, though the camera’s bright flash had clouded my vision a bit. Trevor’s eyes were slits and his mouth was open in laughter. Looking at his narrow face and well-worn blue stocking cap, a sudden sadness came over me. Chad’s aura in the photo was also joyful, his smile infectious. And me—I also looked happy.

“Now just me and Chad,” I said, handing Trevor the camera.

As Trevor fiddled with the device, Chad said to me, "Look over there."

I obliged, wondering what he had noticed this time of night.

"What?" I said, squinting my eyes, not knowing what I was looking for.

"Down that way is where your car broke down, where we came into all the money."

It was true. Just a few miles up the road, on a night that felt as freezing and as abandoned as this one, the three of us had arrived headlong into a fate that no one could have foreseen.

"Life is crazy," I said, putting my arm around him.

"No doubt," Chad agreed.

"You guys ready?" Trevor asked.

"Yep. Take the picture," I told him.

Trevor counted off: "One, two, three."

By the time Trevor was on "three," my hand had become a clenched fist onto the back of Chad's coat collar, pulling him backward. For good measure, I scooped my left arm under his legs and pulled upward, heaving him off the platform like an overlarge fish returning to the ocean. I heard his intake of breath, but there was no screaming on the way down. Just a sickening snap of bone—I hoped it was his neck or perhaps his back—and then silence after his body thudded to the ground.

I peered over the side, anxious. Chad's motionless form was splayed out in an unnatural way, arms and legs akimbo. At the very least he looked badly hurt.

"What do you see down there?" Trevor asked, apparently not wanting to look for himself.

"He's not moving. Come on, let's go down and look."

Trevor handed me the digital camera and followed me downward at a slow pace, opposite of how we'd rushed upward.

When we reached the bottom, I observed Chad for several minutes, trying to decipher if he was dead without having to touch him. Trevor solved the dilemma for me by checking his friend's pulse.

"He's gone," Trevor said.

"Are you sure?"

"Feel for yourself if you want."

"No, I believe you. Are you okay?"

"Not really." He stood up but continued to look at Chad. "You just killed him, Alex. How could I be okay?"

I made no motion to comfort him, to touch him and let him know everything would be all right, just like actors say on TV and in the movies. Truthfully, I wasn't sure myself if anything would ever be okay again. Trevor began sobbing, his shoulders bobbing up and down in an uncontrollable manner. And still I made no move to offer solace. Instead, I pulled out the little white pill that David had given me to kill his wife.

"Take this, Trevor," I said, handing the pill toward him.

His crying stopped and he wiped his nose. "What is it?"

"It'll relax you, buddy. I popped one right before we took the pictures, and I'm already feeling better."

He looked perplexed. "You? You don't take drugs."

"I do tonight," I said, looking down at Chad and shaking my

head. “Hell, I might take another one later.”

Trevor took the pill from me, popping it into his mouth and swallowing. He took a swig from his bottle, which I noticed was Peppermint Schnapps.

There were two park benches stationed at the side of the monumental structure. “Let’s go over there and sit down for a sec,” I said, guiding him toward the benches.

“Shouldn’t we get out of here?”

That’s exactly what I wanted to do, but I had to be patient. “We will, don’t worry. No one’s out here. We’re safe for now.”

We sat down on the cold bench.

“So sad, this whole thing,” Trevor slurred after several minutes. “If we had never met David, none of this ridiculousness would have ever happened. We just killed someone, for God’s sake. A friend.”

“Yes, we did just kill someone, but try to think of it in a positive light, Trevor. If we’d never gotten this money, you and I wouldn’t have become as close. Right?”

He shrugged his shoulders. "I guess. Seems like a hell of a way to become close to your brother. We should have just joined a bowling league or something."

I chuckled. Not long afterward, Trevor started to get woozy, mumbling unformulated words and nodding off, only to lift his head back up in desperation. "Blurry's my vision," he mumbled at one incoherent point.

Then he nodded off for good, and I knew the whole thing was a done deal. Both of them were dead, and on the off chance that they weren't, the freezing temperature would kill them soon enough. I collected myself and scanned the gravel rocks, attempting to smooth out the footsteps and then realizing I was just creating more footsteps. I was being paranoid, I knew, since the rocks showed footsteps all over, but I was looking at it from the viewpoint of sharp authority figures investigating a fishy scene.

I jogged to my car, put on some gloves, and grabbed the plastic grocery bag that had more alcohol. On the way back to the playground, I opened and emptied several cans of beer and half a bottle of vodka on the ground.

When I was back at the scene of the crime, I tossed the empty cans and bottle about in a scattered fashion near both dead bodies. I hadn't touched any of these items all night, so I knew my fingerprints weren't on them. Trevor's bottle was near him on the bench, and Chad's bottle was on the top level of the structure, which I liked—it made it seem like two terrible, drunken accidents had occurred. The extra beer cans and bottle of vodka were mere props in a sad night of debauchery that had ended with deadly results for both men. I slipped a small, unopened bottle of Scotch into Chad's pocket, burrowing it deep inside.

As I stood back up, I turned to my right and saw a lone stick that was about four inches long, wedged into the gravel rocks and standing straight up, a singular entity—a one-stand cross. On a whim I picked it up, walked over to Trevor, and placed it on his knee. I didn't want to cry but was near to bursting.

Looking the area over one more time, I decided everything looked appropriately random and tragic. I trotted back to my car with the empty grocery bag shoved in my pocket, feeling stealthy but knowing I was now a two-time murderer. I started the engine, flipped on the headlights, and drove home.

Chapter 12

It was near midnight when I entered my house as a new man, my head dizzy with measures I'd need to take to erase my presence among Trevor and Chad. Standing inside the laundry room, I stripped naked and gathered up my clothes, which included a belt, my winter coat, and my well-worn Clarks shoes. With the pile in my arms and a box of matches in my hand, I walked to the fireplace in the living room and dropped the load onto the brick mantel.

The glass doors of the fireplace squeaked as I slid them open, probably rusty and inflexible after being motionless for so long. I had to give the chains on both sides of the mesh screen a tough tug so they would open, and then I ducked my head inside the fireplace for a closer look. The sides and grate were tarred black, but the floor was remarkably untouched looking.

I stuffed my shirt, jeans, jacket, T-shirt, and socks inside, and then remembered we had lighter fluid in the garage. I went to get it and then made sure the flue of the fireplace was open. The whole thing lit up in a glorious blaze after throwing in just one lit match. Once good and hot, I fed the fire my shoes and slid in my leather belt. The flames gave off an intense heat and burned everything with a ferocity that was entrancing. I'd used too much lighter fluid, and a noticeable odor that reminded me of a campfire was stinking up the living room. Nonetheless, the heat felt good on my naked body, and I absorbed it for what seemed like a long time, sitting with my legs crossed on the carpet, reaching in to stoke the fire with the iron poker every so often.

I masturbated in front of the fireplace, unable to control the sudden urge.

When the flames died down and nothing much was left except flitting sparks that drifted upward and a significant pile of ashes—which I made a mental note to vacuum later—I roused myself up and headed into the kitchen.

Observing the remnants of our night together was difficult. A neatly stacked deck of cards sat on the kitchen table, a remainder of games played by two people who would never again engage in such a lighthearted activity—in *any* activity, for that matter. I threw away the mostly full bags of chips and pretzels. There were glasses everywhere, and it struck me as wasteful that Trevor had used a fresh one each time he'd served Chad.

I collected all of them and other used dishes and put them in the dishwasher. Though the dishwasher was only half full, I poured extra detergent in both compartments and let it rip. The swishy, watery sound the machine made was like a tonic as I began my cleaning frenzy.

With disinfecting wipes in hand, I snapped items up—anything the two of them may have touched—and wiped them down and put them in cupboards. I sterilized the kitchen counter with the wipes and cleaned the stereo and even the chairs they had sat on, making everything as pristine as possible. I even used the disinfecting wipes to sanitize the spots on the couch where Trevor and Chad had sat.

I returned to the fireplace and wiped the outside of the mantel so that it was clean of any minute fibers or hairs that may have strayed from my clothes, knowing there were likely still some in the house—their DNA and mine, somehow, someway, intermingling.

Next, I dragged out the vacuum and vacuumed the wood floor of the kitchen, going over it as if it were drowning in a sea of dust bunnies. I then vacuumed the entire downstairs as well as the couch and chairs in the family room, where the two of them had played music with such carefree abandon. When the sweeping was completed, I inserted a new bag inside the vacuum cleaner and threw the old one into the garbage. I left the vacuum cleaner in the living room to use in the morning, when the fireplace would be cooled down and I could vacuum the ashes.

By the time I looked at the clock it was three a.m., and like a man possessed, I was still itching to cleanse my house of all outside inhabitants that would lead to trouble if their clues drifted back to me.

Still naked, I went upstairs and climbed into the shower, savoring the cleanness of my house and now my body as I let the steam engulf me and hot water spill all over me for ten minutes.

Then I went to bed and slept ... and dreamt.

It was a warm and gusty summer evening, and darkness was approaching. I sat in the middle of a football field, next to my friend Rory, a baseball teammate of mine from high school. A large group sat among us, one guy a basketball player, a sport I'd never played. Rory and I sat on the ground with our knees clasped to our chests, absorbing the stern lecture being given by Coach Mabry, a taskmaster if there ever was one. His tirade to the team was making me despondent.

At some point the disparaging remarks ended and the group disbanded. I walked off the field, near tears, thinking of Emily and how much I needed her. Oddly, there was a doorbell ringing on the field, a familiar, pleasing sound. It rang and rang, lulling me downward. I wondered if Emily was nearby.

And then something hard and round, like a rock, pounded me on the face. I opened my eyes and jumped up, disoriented.

Trevor was standing by the side of the bed—he looked like he'd risen from the dead.

Before I had a chance to fully absorb the stinging on my face, he lunged at me with both arms out, resembling a zombie out for blood.

"Trevor!" I said, but my words were cut short. He was straddling me, his fingers clenched around my neck, his thumbs pressed into my throat. I couldn't breathe.

Using all the strength I had in my legs and hips, I bucked him upward and heaved my body to the left, holding onto Trevor as I did so. We both fell off the bed and landed on the floor with a crash. I rolled on top of Trevor and reached back to slug him, like he'd slugged me, but then saw the terror in his eyes. I was bigger and stronger and could have pummeled my brother's face into a pulp in no time. He started coughing like crazy, so I jumped up to give him space. "What the fuck, Trevor!"

He was breathing hard and his face was beet red. "Why?" he croaked.

"Why what?" I asked, knowing what had spurred his vengeance.

"You left me in the park. You tried to kill me."

"That's not … that's not true. You passed out. I had to get out of there."

"The pill you gave me. What was it?"

His voice was faltering. I kneeled down to be closer to him. "I'm sorry. I shouldn't have."

He quit talking and closed his eyes. Had he passed out?

I scooted backward and rested my back and head against the door of the closet, breathing as if I'd just jogged three miles. I remembered how we'd given Trevor a key to our house in the past so he could pick up our mail and water our plants when we left town. I never imagined he'd use it for the purpose of entering our house and trying to choke the life out of me.

As I reached into his pocket to retake our key from his keyring, I noticed the light on his cell phone was blinking—he had several unanswered calls. I slipped the phone into my pocket.

Then I closed my eyes and wondered what in the hell I was going to do.

Trevor stayed motionless on the floor, giving me time to think. If Trevor was alive and woke up, what would he do? Try to kill me again? Rat me out? Rat all of us out? Spill the beans entirely so that the money would no longer be mine?

I pushed away the thoughts, wondering if the potency of the pill David had given me had been measured out for an old, dying woman instead of a full-grown man in his prime. Maybe that's why it hadn't killed Trevor.

I crawled over to Trevor and leaned close to his face. His breathing was shallow. I smacked him with force on the cheek a few times, trying to revive him. He moaned a little but didn't stir.

Maybe it was best to get him in my trunk and just drive.

Getting Trevor downstairs and into the car wasn't an easy task. I dragged him by both his arms from our bedroom to the top of the stairs and then had to take a break, out of breath and cursing.

From there, I turned Trevor around and grabbed his arms again, pulling upward so as not to bump his head on the stairs. I descended with caution, looking backward at each step before proceeding so I didn't stumble.

We made it to the bottom. Sliding him on the wood floor was much easier, though I had to take a break in the kitchen because my arms were on fire. Several minutes later, with Trevor comatose on the floor of the laundry room, I walked out to the garage and opened my trunk. I came back in and lifted Trevor by his arms again, easing him out of the doorway. He wasn't a heavy guy, but all this lifting and pulling was going to make me sore tomorrow.

Finagling my brother into the trunk was the toughest task of all, and I almost gave up and put him in the backseat. Trevor was around six feet tall and didn't look comfortable stuffed in my trunk, but I didn't care since he was out cold. Once he was tucked in there as best as I could manage, I closed the trunk, wondering if he would have enough oxygen.

I clicked on the garage door opener in my car and looked in the rearview mirror. There was a cop car in the driveway, and the officer was getting out of his vehicle.

After feeling my heart skip a few beats, I steadied myself and got out to greet him. The guy looked like a cop's cop with his starched uniform, dark sunglasses, jutting jaw with no chin fat, and dark hair peeking out from underneath his hat. He was trim and muscular and looked to be in his twenties or early thirties.

"Howdy," I said. "Everything okay? Didn't expect to see a police car in my driveway."

He took off his hat, scratched his head, and removed his sunglasses. He had piercing blue eyes and a full head of hair, probably a real heartbreaker with the ladies.

"I'm real sorry to bug ya on a Saturday, Mr. Neitzel. Truly am. My name's Officer Dovis. Wanted to ask ya a few questions."

His voice was high-pitched and uncertain. The guy sounded like a total hick, not at all like the James Bond type of crime-solver I thought he'd be. "Yeah, sure. Would you like to come inside?"

"No, out here'll do. What happened to your face?"

I stared at him blankly and then remembered. "Oh, this!" I answered, touching the wound. "Knocked the hell out of it last night when I got up to go to the bathroom, still half asleep. Banged my head against the edge of the bathroom door. Sadly, it's not the first time that's happened."

He regarded me for a moment and then said, "Need to watch yourself. Looks pretty red."

"Well, it'll heal. It doesn't hurt that bad."

"Kind of a bump there."

"Yeah. It's not that bad."

"If you say so. Your wife here?"

"She's out of town. Went up north to see her parents."

"Oh. Well, listen, do you know of a guy named Chad Batt?"

I pretended to think for a second. "Uh, yes, I do, actually. He's friends with my brother if I'm not mistaken."

"That's why I'm here. He's been found dead in Cameron Park, and we're looking for some of his friends to see what may have happened. Do you know where your brother is?"

"I don't, I'm sorry."

"Understand. We've been trying to reach him and haven't had any luck. Also haven't been able to find him at his apartment. When's the last time you saw him?"

"Man, let me think. Um, he came by the house a week ago. He was here for a few hours on a Saturday. We just caught up, that sort of thing."

"Uh-hu. Anything seem out of sorts with him? Was he okay at the time? I mean, mentally and all that."

"As far as I could tell, though he did mention he was having relationship problems with, well, Chad."

"Chad Batt?"

"Yeah."

"What did he specifically say?"

"Uh, well, I know they were on the outs. Chad had broken up with him, and my brother was upset. I didn't get too many details."

"Uh-hu. Okay. Did he say anything else to you that day, anything that stands out?"

"Not really. We had some coffee, talked for a bit, watched TV, and then he left. That's the last time I remember talking to him."

"Okay. Do me a favor, will ya? Call me if you hear from him." He handed me his card. "We're looking to see what he might know about Chad Batt's death, if anything."

"Sure, of course."

"I'll be in touch with you if I have any further questions."

"Yes, that sounds good. I'm sorry to hear about Chad. How did he die?"

"Looks to have fallen from that playground thing at the park. Or he was pushed. We don't know." The cop tipped his hat at me and climbed into his car. At that very moment, I could hear Trevor knocking the inside of my trunk, yelling to be let out.

I got in my car and drove to the north end of town to a desolate spot I knew of. Trevor had stopped banging around and yelling in the back, maybe because he knew he was being driven somewhere.

I drove into a seedy-looking neighborhood off Bradley Avenue and kept taking lefts and rights until I found an area I'd driven past but never into. Set away from the neighborhood I'd gone through, it was nothing more than a wide expanse of gravel rocks with brown grass intersecting them down the middle. Off in the distance some warehouses and decrepit buildings gave the grounds a semblance of atmosphere. I kept driving until I came to a rise in the rocks where train tracks were. I parked and got out of the car, looking all around to make sure I was alone.

I popped the trunk open, half expecting Trevor to leap out at me and start strangling me again, but he'd passed out once more.

Or maybe he'd died. Either way, he was ghost white. Wearing gloves, I yanked him up and dragged him out, pulling him onto the train tracks.

"Trevor," I said, wondering if I could rouse him. His eyes remained closed, so I pulled out a pocket knife and sliced open the veins of his left wrist, cutting at them vertically instead of crosswise. They spurted blood and I set the pocket knife—*his* pocket knife, one that I'd grabbed from his coat pocket last night—by his right side.

Trevor wasn't moving, and I was pretty sure he wasn't going to rise from the dead this time. I jumped back into my car and sped off, conscious I was doing all this in broad daylight.

On the way home, I made a quick stop to a little man-made lake in town, strolling around its perimeter as if I did this sort of thing every wintry day. Making sure I was alone, I reached into my pocket and threw Trevor's phone and pocket knife, one at a time, into the lake.

Chapter 13

When Emily came home from Chicago the next day, she asked me why there was an ashtray full of cigarettes sitting on the counter in our garage. This was after she noticed and asked about the swelling bruise on my face. I'd forgotten all about Trevor and Chad making their unending trips to the garage to smoke their cigs.

"I had a few guys over," I explained.

"Who? You don't hang out with anybody."

I frowned. "That's not true. I invited some guys from work over. We played cards."

"*Who*?"

"You've never met them, Emily. We had a few beers is all, played some poker."

"I didn't even know you knew *how* to play poker. Did you win any money?"

"No, not really."

"Are you *sure* you didn't get into a fight or something? That bump on your face is really nasty."

"I didn't get into a fight, Em. I told you what happened."

"Yeah, you ran into the door in the middle of the night. So weird."

"I told you, I was tipsy."

Emily crossed her arms and looked around the kitchen. "Well, at least you cleaned up. The place looks great."

"Thanks. I didn't want you to have to worry about anything when you got back."

The air purifier had sucked up the kerosene stink in the living room, and some canned air freshener sweetened the scent of the whole downstairs. Emily joked that I was trying to cover up a wild party, and I kept telling her it was just three guys who'd come over, all of whom were gone by eleven o'clock.

That night my dad called. "Trevor's gone," he stated in a distraught voice.

"What?" I yelled, feigning surprise and acting the part I

needed to as Emily turned to look at me. We were both sitting on the couch watching TV.

“He’s gone, Alex. Ran over by a train on some dirty train tracks on the north side of town. He was sliced right in half. They found his wallet.”

“My God, Dad. I can’t believe it.” And I couldn’t. I’d figured trains didn’t even run over those forlorn old tracks.

“What happened?” Emily whispered. I covered the phone and told her the news. Her mouth dropped open in shock.

“Dad, I’ll be right over, okay?”

“Don’t bother. I’m calling you from the hospital. Your mom is not doing well, Son.”

“Geez. What’s wrong with her?”

“Her lungs are giving out and she’s on a respirator. I don’t know how much longer she’ll last.”

“A respirator? Why didn’t you tell me?”

“Because, Alex, I got the news today that my son died and I had to go ID him, on top of what’s going on with your mom. I can't process all this at once."

"I'm coming to the hospital, okay? I'll be right there."

Emily came with me. We sat in a darkened room for almost six hours, enduring the blips and bleeps of machines and eventually watching a nurse shut off the respirator, seeing Mom expire. All I could think about was that I had no idea she'd taken such a bad turn so quickly, and that I hadn't been around to say a proper goodbye.

Of all things, I felt guilty.

Both funerals were cold, drizzly affairs. I held Emily's hand throughout both of them, sad and stupefied by what I'd become.

Foul play was not suspected in the deaths of my brother and Chad. Nonetheless, a journalistic saga developed: two gay men—former lovers—one found dead in a park and one mutilated by an oncoming train. It was all too good *not* to write about, I guess. Their endings were recognized far and wide as a woeful *Romeo and Juliet* type of drama in which it was speculated that Chad, under the influence of gargantuan amounts of booze, accidentally fell to his death, while my brother, witnessing this horrendous fall, killed himself elsewhere. The fact that there was no corroborating evidence to vindicate this story was beside the point—it made for a gossipy, speculative narrative that was mystifying to boot.

Helpless, I observed the news of Trevor and Chad's ending grow from a morbid local narrative in our homey little newspaper to a much broader audience. When reporters from The Associated Press, *Us* and *People* magazines, as well as countless online news organizations began calling Emily and I nonstop, I knew things had spiraled beyond my control. We never gave them interviews. Poor Emily was blindsided by all of this, and I tried to comfort her amid the chaos as best I could, conscious that she was carrying our baby.

To my advantage, I realized the surrounding tabloid circus would only help my cause, better obscure what really happened.

On the flip side, it occurred to me that one of these

enterprising young reporters, looking to make a name for herself, might scope for something beyond the theoretical and begin digging around my neck of the woods for genuine clues. The thought petrified me, kept me awake for long hours of the night.

But then the hullabaloo dissipated just as fast as it had come crashing in. After getting their banal quotes from Chad and Trevor's friends and writing their pieces and doing their TV spots, the members of the press moved on to the next story somewhere else.

Time went by and nothing of consequence happened, no police interviews, nothing. Emily did her best to stay upbeat, heralding the coming baby as a spark to keep our household flickering with a semblance of optimism and hope. We invited my father over for dinner often, surprised that he accepted most of the time. Our lives went on, and I began to feel less apprehensive that my crimes would be discovered. At times I trekked to the upstairs closet to cipher cash from the suitcase, which Emily was still oblivious to.

One cold morning in late February, I went with a few work colleagues in a company van to Chicago for a business trip. It was pitch black out as the vehicle slogged ahead on the icy highway. Twenty minutes into the trip on I-57 North, I looked out the window and noticed, a few miles away across a sprawling cornfield, a lit-up cross that had tipped over and was perched at a strange angle. The lights outlining the cross held the promise of a new day, but the fallen piece looked united with the pitiful morning.

"Hate to be the one who had to get that thing back in the ground," said a hefty coworker sitting next to me in the back seat. "It's massive. Must be a church."

"Yeah," I agreed, fighting back tears. "Hard to see out there."

I shut my eyes, not wanting to cry, though I'm sure he would have understood. Everyone at work knew what I'd been going through with my brother and mom.

By the time we cruised past Manteno, the day had brightened

and the roads were less hazardous— we arrived in Chicago in one piece. Between meetings, the vision of the cross we'd seen that morning kept popping into my head. When I got home that night, tired from the busy day, I even told Emily about it. She said we should start going to church once the baby was born.

Given my sinful ways, which I hadn't even begun to fully contemplate and come to terms with, who was I to argue?

Chapter 14

November 2006

As sleet came down full force, I pulled into the driveway of Dad's house, my childhood home located in the well-to-do neighborhood of Shady Acres. When we'd first moved here, Shady Acres was a new, sprawling neighborhood that hadn't a substantial tree in sight, no vegetation whatsoever that could provide a lick of shade, making the moniker a running family joke over the years.

But things had changed. Tall trees were now everywhere, some of them hanging over the street like half tunnels, bursting with multicolored leaves that were falling at a fast clip in the gusty wind as sleet pelted my car at a wayward angle.

Dad had met someone and was remarrying in a few months. He and his future wife, Judy, had moved into a new condo not far from the house he still owned, which he'd sold a week ago. Not one to waste time, Dad had sold or gotten rid of the furniture he and Judy didn't need, while the items being kept were already at the new residence. What hadn't been dealt with yet were the odds and ends he'd had for years.

Holding a piping hot cup of coffee in my hand, I got out of the car and tucked in my head while covering my eyes with my hand to stave off the sleet as best I could. I walked inside, grateful for the warmth, hoping this project wouldn't take the entire day.

"This won't take all day," Dad told me right away, perhaps gauging my demeanor. He was wearing scrubby gray sweat pants and a faded sweatshirt he'd gotten in Ireland. Noticing his attire, I felt overdressed in my stylish dark blue jeans and striped brown sweater with a collared button-down underneath.

"I've got things arranged in piles so that we can get through this as painlessly as possible. This pile here," Dad said, pointing at the center of the living room, "is what I consider to be, if not outright junk, then stuff we probably don't want anymore. You can rummage through it to see if you or Emily, or maybe someone else you know, wants any of it."

I eyed the items, not seeing anything of interest at first glance.

"Over here are things we may want to keep, but maybe not. It's kind of the halfway pile, if you will. There's also stuff here that we may want to sell."

"You put a lot of thought into this, Dad."

"Well, I just want to make sure we don't throw away anything important."

He walked over to some items sitting next to the sliding glass door that led to the backyard. "These are things I want to keep. I've also got some stuff in the garage that I want you to look at."

The house, including the entire upstairs, was mostly empty besides these pesky lingering objects, and it dawned on me that this might be the final time I'd ever be inside my old house.

"When's the new family moving in?" I asked.

"Middle of next week. They're coming from Wisconsin."

We began with the "junk" pile. Except for a few picture frames and plant holders that I thought Emily might want, my dad was right: these were things that could either be thrown away or given to Goodwill. We made snappy decisions about each item and soon were putting things in bags so they could go to new destinations. Dad began hauling out the insignificant stuff that neither of us wanted.

The second pile, the one Dad was less certain about, took longer to get through. Indeed, I could understand his indecision over some of the items, many of which had once belonged to my mom. We came across several things Trevor had once owned, making it an even more depressing process. In the end, we decided about half the stuff in the pile was worth splitting up between us and keeping; the other items could be pitched or Dad would try to sell. We divvied up the possessions based mostly on whether Emily or Judy would find them useful.

After about an hour of this, my dad grasped my elbow and said, "Here, look at this." He handed me a colorful-looking scrapbook, which at first I thought had once belonged to Mom. On closer inspection, though, I saw it had been Trevor's. His initials, "TN," made of felt, were glued to the red cover, their vivacious blue color creating a bold, inviting look.

"Did Mom do this for Trevor?"

"No. Your mom's scrapbooks dedicated to you boys are over there," he said, nodding toward the pile of stuff he'd relegated for himself. "But I thought you might want to keep this one since Trevor put it together." Dad, looking down at the floor, seemed to falter for a second. "I know you and him had become closer before he died."

Nodding, I said, "Yeah, I guess that's true." I sat down on a wooden trunk and began flipping through the pages of Trevor's scrapbook. To my surprise, Dad sat down next to me and leaned in close.

"Hold on, go slower," he said. "Start from the beginning. You'll find this interesting, I think."

I turned the pages back to the front of the scrapbook. "When did he start this?"

"I don't know. It's probably something he started in high school and came back to over the years."

The first few pages had an aerial theme going on. A large cutout picture of a commercial jet airliner was on page one, surrounded by cutout snippets of clouds, birds, and skyscrapers, all things high in the air.

"Interesting," I said. "It's well put together."

"Yeah, the next page has other things related to transportation and such."

I flipped the page and observed a picture of a long train glued across both pages, right away making me think of Trevor's ultimate end and my part in it. It was an Amtrak train, and surrounding it was filth and debris, nothing but garbage. Some of the images were cut out of magazines, but a lot of them were sketched in by Trevor in an amorphous way, as if the magazine photos and Trevor's drawings had melded together and were now one. There was a stop sign planted at the train's front end, which I thought was a creative idea. Unlike the peppy, high-flying first page, complete with blue skies and all things upward, this page contained smog in the background, objects that produced a foul stench.

Flipping forward, I came to a page that was aquatic in nature; another few pages ahead showed multiple helicopters, swarming together like spindly insects high in the air; and then we came to an extensive section where he had combined upbeat images with the darker side of life. One page featured an illustration of a red heart, but within it were oily-looking snakes crawling around in a haphazard fashion. Elsewhere, cute little girls showcased ink-penned tattoos on their faces, ones drawn by Trevor; ice cream cones dripped blood instead of vanilla; cheerleaders wore sneering expressions and held deflated basketballs in their clenched hands; an Easter bunny that wasn't posing with a dopey, buck-toothed smile, but instead possessed razor-sharp teeth and a sinister expression that made you look away; a female anorexic Santa Claus exposing her miniscule breasts; and on it went for the next few pages.

"Weird," I said.

"Your brother had a phase when he was a little bit depressed,

I think," Dad said. "It gets weirder."

And indeed, it did. Turning the pages—and lingering for less time on each one as I did so—I recalled that Trevor had at one time gone through a wild drug phase with his friends. I think Dad and I were witnessing some of the byproducts of that period.

It started off innocently enough with pasted pictures of such bands as the Sex Pistols, Buzzcocks, Ramones, Red Hot Chili Peppers, X, Hüsker Dü, and more obscure bands I hadn't heard of. Screaming, angry young men, some of them pimply with flushed faces and Mohawks or wild hair meant to make a statement. Bass guitars were held askew, the cords of microphones snaked about on stages, and roughshod-looking drums blended into the backgrounds.

I flipped ahead, anxious to see where things were going.

The pages became depraved: a dour moonlit scene in 1930s England where a rape was occurring; blood gushing from the mouth of what looked to be a war-torn child; a blind man whose cane had been stolen from him by a group of heckling teenagers with shaved heads; a dead dog on the side of a road, surrounded on one side by people pointing and laughing, one maniacal guy with a bloody knife in his hand.

I wondered what had made Trevor see the world this way. "Was Trevor really so sad and … warped?" I asked my father.

"He wasn't warped, Alex. I think this was just an expression for him, his outlet."

I turned from the scrapbook to look at him. "Why would you think I would like this, Dad?"

He tilted his head and thought about my question for a second. "I don't know. I guess because it came from your brother."

"Well, he was a creative guy, I'll give him that."

"Not all of it is bleak. Let me see it for a second. I'll show you the end. That's the part that's most interesting to me."

Dad flipped to the back of the scrapbook, where a big green dollar sign took up the entire page; underneath it were large capitalized block letters that read MONEY, MONEY, MONEY,

MONEY, MONEY, MONEY!

"Hmm," I said, caught off guard.

"Yeah, he gets a tad money hungry here. And look at this," Dad said, flipping to the next page and pointing to it. On the page, Trevor had cut out credos and quotes meant to inspire: *Be all you can be*; "*There is nothing in the universe that I fear but that I shall not know all my duty, or shall fail to do it.*" (Mary Lyon, an American educator); "*Our chief defect is that we are more given to talking about things than to doing them.*" (Jawaharlal Nehru, Indian statesman). There was an illustration of half of a rainbow connected to a pot of gold. This last section had a more contained, elegant feel compared to what we'd looked at earlier. I absorbed the images slowly.

"You can see he clearly had some dreams," Dad said. "I didn't know until looking through this that he wanted to go to California and be a manager for famous people."

"What?"

"Yeah," Dad said, turning the page in an excited way. Trevor had cut out and pasted some of Hollywood's biggest stars and outlined them in various colors in crayon, creating a rainbow effect that enhanced their whitened teeth and radiant smiles even more. Lots of male actors and musicians were plastered on the pages, some dating back to the graceful black-and-white years when Cary Grant and Marilyn Monroe had ruled the world. There was also lots of Elvis and Johnny Cash.

"How do you know he wanted to manage famous people?" I asked.

"Look here," Dad said, turning to the final page. On it, Trevor had created two "Most Wanted" lists, one listing established stars and another one with "up and coming" Hollywood starlets and wannabe heartthrobs. Next to Julia Roberts' name he'd written, "Just the type I'd like to manage."

"I think that managing people was his dream," Dad said.

"Maybe." I snapped the scrapbook shut. "That was pretty intense."

"Hang onto it, Alex. You'll be glad you did, and I think he

would have wanted you to have it. I've got other stuff of Trevor's for keepsakes."

We forged ahead for another few hours, sorting through items in the garage and in the kitchen, taking breaks and chatting from time to time. Dad kept trying to pawn off various-sized wood planks and tools he had in the garage, none of which I had any use for.

"You want to get some lunch?" he asked after we'd finally gotten through it all. He was pulling off his work gloves, which made me notice how dirty my hands were from not wearing any. "It's my treat."

I told him yes and we agreed on meeting at a Mexican place in thirty minutes since he wanted to stop by his condo to change.

"Say goodbye, Alex. You probably won't be here again. Be sure to lock the front door before you leave." He patted me on the back and left.

Alone now, I realized this really was it—a departure from a big part of my former life. It certainly made sense for Dad to sell the place. He and Judy didn't need all this space, and half the members of his immediate family—the people who had resided here with him—were dead. It was possible that the house had become a source of sorrow for my dad, though he'd never said as much to me.

I strolled through every single room one final time, thinking of things that had happened in each one. I ended up in my parents' bedroom, remembering their large bed, the familial comfort of their presence. With no actual bed to sit on, I plunked down on the hardwood floor and pulled my knees to my chest, all at once sobbing, blubbering about how I wished I could go back in time, words no one would ever hear.

Several minutes later I stopped and could hear the wind blowing outside. Breathing hard and shaken, I leaned back on the bare floor and stretched out on my back, resting my eyes, wanting to disappear. After a while I pulled myself up off the floor and walked to the bedroom window, where I watched a large crow come swooping down onto a tree branch in my parents' yard—and then, *SNAP*, the branch went down. The crow fluttered in the air for a second, getting its bearings, and then flapped its wings and flew off, maybe in search of a sturdier perch to rest on.

Feeling drained, I went into the living room and then the garage to gather up all the items I'd be taking with me, including Trevor's scrapbook. It took several trips to get everything in the car, and I was late meeting my dad.

Chapter 15

Lunch with Dad had improved my mood a little, and I was looking forward to spending the rest of the day on the couch, maybe finding a good movie.

Emily happened to be sitting on the couch with her legs resting on the coffee table when I walked in the family room. She was reading a magazine, like usual. A cup of steaming hot tea sat on the table with a spoon in it and the string of the tea bag hanging out. She barely looked up at me. “Hey,” I said, sitting down on a chair by the couch.

“Hey. How’d it go?”

I thought about it for a second. “Kind of depressing, to be honest.”

Emily didn’t respond; she just kept reading. Earlier it had crossed my mind that maybe we could look at Trevor’s scrapbook together, but now that idea seemed ridiculous—Emily wouldn’t want to see that side of Trevor.

“I put some boxes in the garage of stuff I kept,” I said, trying to engage her. “You can look through them if you want.”

“Okay.”

“I’ll put them in the garage attic later.”

A slight nod from Emily.

“The boxes, I mean.”

“Yeah.”

“Emily.”

She looked up from her magazine. “What?”

“Maybe we should talk.”

She placed the magazine on her lap.

“We can’t go on like this. I miss how things used to be. Don’t you?”

“What?”

“Miss how things used to be. Are you not listening to me?”

She sighed. “I am.”

“It doesn’t seem like it. Look, I’m not asking you to get over what happened tomorrow. I’ve never once not let you grieve. I know it’s a process that’ll take time. A lot of time. *I’m* still getting over it."

Emily didn't say anything.

"Maybe we could take a vacation, go somewhere. Anywhere."

"That's your solution to everything."

"I'm just trying to help."

"I'm tired of traveling."

"What do you want then, Emily? How can I make things better?"

Emily looked at me for a long time. Finally, she tossed the magazine on the coffee table and stood up. "I'll be right back."

I heard her go upstairs, and at first I didn't think she was coming back; it took her more than ten minutes to return to the family room. When she did, she was holding something I couldn't see. She walked toward where I was sitting, holding the item behind her back, looking down at me, again peering into my eyes. She seemed to be deciding whether or not she even wanted to proceed.

"What?" I asked.

Emily held out her hand and showed me the digital camera. I hadn't seen it for a long time, had actually forgotten all about it. I shifted in the chair. "Yeah, so?"

She turned the camera on. I could hear a few soft bleeps as she hit a few buttons on it. Then she turned the camera around and presented the picture of me, Trevor, and Chad, the one from Cameron Park.

I looked at her and said, "Yeah, I remember that photo. It's a good one."

That brought a smirk to her face. "Is that all you've got to say?"

"What? Yeah, I guess so. What, Emily?" I was starting to get nervous.

"You realize, don't you, that the exact day and time this photo was taken is on the camera."

"Um, I guess so."

Emily was smiling now, but it wasn't an endearing smile. She was getting impatient. "Is there anything you want to tell me,

Alex?"

"Well, I don't like how mysterious you're being. It's a photo, Emily. So what?"

"*So* it was taken at eleven thirty-two p.m. on the night I was at my parents' house for the weekend, right before Chad and Trevor were found dead."

"Okay."

"You never said anything about seeing Chad and Trevor that night. You told me you had friends from work over at our house."

"I did."

"So why am I looking at, right now, Alex, a photo of you and Trevor and Chad from that same night, a night that you told me everyone had left our house by eleven?"

"We went out to the bars, Emily. I saw Trevor and Chad out, and we took that picture."

"Oh, really? You didn't say anything about going to the bars. Why did you keep that from me?"

"I thought you might be mad."

"Mad at you for going out with your friends to the bars?"

"Yeah."

Her smirk was long gone and now she was just angry. "Here's what I'm getting at, Alex: I find it weird that on the night before both your brother and Chad were found dead soon after, it didn't occur to you to tell me that you'd seen them that weekend."

I sat there stunned and angry that I'd forgotten all about the digital camera and failed to delete the goddammed photo. Emily had used that camera all the time back then, and it was careless of me not to think of that. "I don't have to sit here and listen to this," I said, standing up and walking away. "I don't know what you're accusing me of, but I don't like it."

As I was stalking out of the room, Emily said, "I talked to the police, Alex."

I turned around. "What?"

"Back when all that happened. The cops came by here when you weren't around. They wanted to know what you were doing that night, and what I was doing."

"What did you say?"

Emily stalled for a second, I think enjoying watching my discomfort. "I bailed you out, Alex. I gave you a somewhat decent alibi."

"What?"

"I told them you took me to Peotone that night so we could meet my parents halfway to Chicago, and that we had a late dinner there. We used to do that sometimes, so I thought it was a legitimate thing to say. I always thought they'd come back to you—or maybe even my parents—to try to verify my story independently, but they never did."

"Why would you do that, Emily? You could have gotten into serious trouble for lying."

She started to say something and then stopped. "The bottom line is that I saw the photo not long after Trevor and Chad both died, and then saw the date and time. I had this gut feeling that something wasn't right. So when the cops came by, I decided to try to protect you."

"Protect me from what?"

"What do you think, Alex? This picture!" She jerked the camera closer to my face for emphasis. "The full ashtray in the garage, which was weird, just so unlike you. I thought it was suspicious when you said a few of your friends from work were out there smoking, but I knew Trevor *for sure* smoked."

I walked to the couch and sat down. "It wasn't Trevor. It was my work friends smoking out there."

"Come on, Alex. What about that red bump on your face? That was the weirdest thing of all. You said you knocked your head against the bathroom door, but it looked like something worse than that. It looked like you'd gotten in a fight."

"Did the cops suspect me of doing something?"

"I'm not sure. Maybe. They left us alone after that, so obviously they thought I was telling the truth. But I put my ass on the line for you, Alex. I mean, I could go to jail for lying if any of this ever comes out."

"I know that. So why'd you do it? Tell me."

"Because … you're my husband. We had a baby on the way. We had a life planned out. Now all of that's gone to shit."

"Emily."

"No, don't try to comfort me!" Emily put her hands over her face, trying to compose herself. "Just tell me what happened that night, Alex. You owe me that."

I was tired of the whole charade, so I told her everything, starting with meeting David Kendrick, which she already knew about. I then told her about the five-million-dollar offer he'd put forth, how he'd died right in front of me with the money right there, and how I'd done nothing to help him. I told her about how I'd been hoarding the money all this time and where it was in our house.

I was honest about the night we'd taken the photo on the digital camera and where the three of us actually were. She was in shock when I told her what I did to Chad, and she squirmed with disgust as I told her about leaving Trevor all bloodied up on the train tracks. She began crying, but I didn't stop. I filled her in on the conniving, insecure way I'd behaved, and told her about my constant concerns about Chad being a liability where the money was concerned. I left nothing out.

And then I watched her walk away, dazed.

I remained on the couch long after Emily left the room, falling asleep on my back in short spurts that were punctuated by loud snorts that jolted me awake. Sleeping on my back was never a good idea. I'd gained a fair amount of weight the past few years, and sleep apnea seemed to be one of the effects of that. Emily told me I woke up a lot, though I wondered how she knew that, given that we'd been sleeping in separate bedrooms for months now.

Our marriage had been strained ever since Emily had carried and delivered our stillborn baby. When the doctor told us it was safe to start trying for a pregnancy again, I'd noticed some reluctance on Emily's part, which confused me. Nonetheless, as months slipped by and we couldn't get pregnant again, I'd secretly used some of my hidden stash upstairs to pay for in vitro fertilization, which Emily had seemed somewhat excited about. When that process failed, our sex life became nonexistent. For the past few years I'd chalked up Emily's sullen mood toward me—and toward life in general—to the stillborn child and our childless future.

Until today. I now realized that Emily's repulsion toward me was because of what she'd pieced together about that fateful night with Trevor and Chad.

Sighing, I looked at the coffee table to my right and saw the magazine Emily had been reading earlier, a copy of *Vanity Fair*. Opening it up, I came to an article about a former magazine writer. The piece began:

When Richard James sleeps at night, he dreams of how he can help people. Then he wakes to write down what he just dreamt about, making sure to capture as many details as possible. It's a strange way of slumbering that has defined James's life for years.

"I was put on this earth to do good things, and I do those good deeds through my writing," said a smiling James, his cup of steaming Starbucks coffee clasped in his large hands.

The trouble is, much of what James has written about for Ebony *magazine during the past year and a half has been patently false, made-up narratives of superhero financial wizards who assisted fictitious individuals of all ages who were trying to improve their economic situations.*

Many of these published stories, in fact, stemmed from James's late-night visions.

The article was so riveting that I didn't notice Emily standing right next to me until she cleared her throat. I placed the magazine on my chest. "Hey," I said.

She stood there, not saying anything. So I waited.

"I remember how secretive you were with Trevor not long before he died," she began. "You two would talk, and it always seemed like I was intruding. And I remember now how often you went into the upstairs closet. You once told me it was because you were fixing that shelf in there."

I smiled, remembering that I'd paid someone to fix the shelf.

"But it was because the money was in that humongous suitcase, which I never bothered to open. All the traveling we've done, and we never took that suitcase. Now I know why."

Emily had been behind me, but she took a few steps forward and turned to look down, straight into my eyes. "And the large bills that are always in your pocket. The overpriced car you bought for yourself. Always going out to eat for dinner. Tons of nice gifts that you've given me over the years. How could I have been so oblivious?"

"Emily, you should know I've been super careful. I don't flaunt that money nearly as much as some people would. I've continued to work. I never pay all cash for big-ticket items."

Emily crossed her arms and looked away from me. "Wow. You're such a saint."

I sat up on the couch. "No one ever needs to know about this.

We could still have a great life together despite my mistakes. We could move far away from here. It's not too late."

Emily snickered. "It *is* too late, Alex. I want you to leave. And take that suitcase with you. I want it out of here."

I stood up and walked toward her; she walked backward, a frightened look on her face. "Emily, I love you. I'm so sorry I never told you about all this. It just never seemed like the *right* time to tell you. I never knew how to bring it up. It was hard, you know?"

"I want you out of here. I want a divorce. You'd better get a lawyer, and you'd better not fight any of this. There's a load of things I now know about you that I'm guessing you'd rather keep quiet. I'm not going to tell anyone, but don't test me."

I nodded, humbled and on the verge of tears. "Okay then."

Emily started to walk away and then stopped to face me again. "You scare me, Alex. I feel like I don't even know you. To be so motivated by money to do those things, to kill … it scares me beyond belief. How could you do all that?"

“I did it for us, Em.”

A sarcastic laugh seemed to escape from her throat. “Please leave by tonight. Don’t make this hard.”

She was walking away again when I said, “Why have you stayed with me, Emily? I mean, if you suspected certain things, why didn’t you just talk to me about it much sooner, confront me?”

Emily, with her back to me, paused for a second. “Part of it was because of the baby. I just couldn’t deal with any more drama after what happened. I didn’t have the will or energy. I was too sad.” She turned around to look at me a final time. “But the other part of it, I have to admit, is because you’ve always been a good provider. And now I know why.”

That evening I found a hotel on the outskirts of town, where I lived for the next several months.

Chapter 16

One evening after work, not long after spending Thanksgiving alone, I wandered into a used-goods store at Country Lane Shopping Center, not far from the bus stop where I'd picked up Chad and Trevor a few years ago.

An old lady was cashiering up front, sitting on a stool behind the counter. I gave her a nod. She was sketching something, her hand holding a pencil and moving it about in an assured manner.

I'd always liked the name of the store, Junction Junk, as well as the quality of items it sold, so I tried to support it every now and again. It was a sizable place with tall shelves that held varied merchandise people donated. Emily and I had given the store many unneeded household items over the years, things such as clothing, old board games, blankets, and jackets.

I scanned the aisles. "Do you have pocket knives?" I asked the lady.

"I think aisle two, near the kitchenware and silverware." Her voice had a hardened rasp, as if she'd once been a smoker or maybe still was.

I told her thanks and walked to aisle two. She was right about the location, but I was uninspired by the selection of knives. With my hands in my pockets, I strolled through all the aisles of Junction Junk. Certain things caught my attention: I saw a small-screened DVD player that was kind of cool; they had a nice selection of sports coats, sunglasses, and short-sleeved Polo shirts, one of which I took off the rack to purchase; I also looked through the CDs and paintings. I was the only person in the store and in no hurry.

I approached the counter to pay for the shirt. "Quiet here tonight," I said to the lady.

"It often is. Is this all for you?"

"Yeah, this is it," I replied, handing her the shirt. "You guys close every night at seven?"

"I believe on Saturdays we stay open until eight. I could be wrong, though. My mind can get a little off track these days."

Standing right next to her, I could see just how old she was.

Her sunken, weather-beaten face contained a highway of crisscrossed lines, and her white hair was wispy and balding. But the woman had pretty arched eyebrows and beautiful blue eyes that sparkled—eyes similar to Emily's. I looked at her nametag: Phyllis Kendrick.

I couldn't stop staring. Phyllis Kendrick. My hands were pressed hard against the counter and my heart was thudding in my chest. The woman was saying something to me. "What?" I said.

"I said I was right. We close at eight p.m. on Saturdays. I looked it up."

"Oh. Thanks."

"Are you okay, sir?"

"Yes. Sorry."

"It's seven dollars for the shirt."

I handed her a ten-dollar bill and said, "What are you drawing?" My heart was still thumping and I was trying to calm myself by focusing on something else.

“Oh, this?” she said, looking down at her sketch. She turned it around so I could see. “Here, take a look.”

The forefront of the picture was of a hill with rolling hillsides in the background, different from the landscape in central Illinois. Even though it was the centerpiece of the sketch, the hill had a faraway feel to it. The top portion of the picture, where there was sky, was penciled in at a darker shade, making it look as if nightfall was approaching.

“This is great,” I told her.

“Oh, why, thank you. I sometimes give my drawings away, but I paste most of them into a scrapbook-journal at home. Whenever I’m gone another soul can hopefully enjoy them.”

I pointed at the top of the hill and asked, “Is that a tombstone?”

“Yes, it is.”

“What’s the significance of it, if you don’t mind my asking?”

“No, I don’t mind. I just like drawing tombstones. It’s not the location we buried Jared at. That was my son. We buried him here because this is home. We moved here from the Chicago suburbs years ago."

"I'm sorry about your son."

"Thank you. He died a long time ago."

I stuck out my hand. "My name's Alex."

She shook it and said, "Phyllis. But I guess you saw that from my nametag, which you were really staring at."

"I'm sorry about that."

She laughed. "It's okay."

"I thought maybe I knew you is all."

"Me?"

"Or maybe your husband. Your last name sounds familiar."

"Well, his first name was David. He's passed on, too."

"Sorry to hear that as well. David Kendrick. I don't think I knew him."

"He was a doctor and started a pharmaceutical company."

"Ah. Sounds like a sharp guy."

"And a rich guy. After he died, his accountant discovered five million dollars that was missing from his financial portfolio."

My chest got tight again and the thudding resumed. "Wow. What happened to it?"

"No one knows because it's gone. Poof!" she said with a glint in her eyes and a wave of her frail, spotty hand. She peered into my eyes, giving me the creeps.

"Well, do you think they'll find out what happened to it?"

"I do, yes."

"Yeah? How?"

"Because it's five million dollars. They won't quit until they find the culprit."

"The culprit?"

"Yes. I believe it was stolen."

"Oh? Why do you think that?"

"I was very sick for a long time, and that's about the time the money went missing. I believe that David was careless and that somehow the money was taken from us."

"But … how could anyone just *take* that much money?"

"David had a lot of wheelings and dealings going on when he was alive. They'll find it." Phyllis gave me my change and asked if I had kids.

"Me? Oh, no. My wife and I tried, but it just never worked out for us. We're getting a divorce, unfortunately."

"Sorry to hear that. My marriage wasn't peaches and cream either, if it makes you feel any better."

"You said you were sick for a while?" I asked, wanting to change the subject and curious about how she'd recovered from such poor health.

I could tell Phyllis enjoyed relating how she'd fought leukemia for several years, along with a host of other health-related crises that came with it, and won the battles. If the story hadn't come from a woman who I'd once been asked to kill, and whose husband hadn't perished of a heart attack right in front of me, it would have been a supremely inspiring tale. But given my undisclosed linked past with this formerly sick lady—I was having a hard time reconciling that I'd stumbled into her—it was hard to believe her presence was even real. David had pronounced her as good as dead only a few years ago.

"How did your son die?" I asked, after she'd stopped talking about her illnesses.

It took her a few moments to answer. "Well, first off, he was autistic, which wasn't always easy for David and me."

"Sure."

"Jared's autism was a real shock to us both. I'm not sure if you've ever encountered an autistic child or adult extensively, but it can take some getting used to, some ... adjustments."

"Yeah, I'm sure."

"But lucky for us, David was a physician in the early years, and he knew a lot about it—and what he didn't know he studied up on. He knew, for instance, that certain antipsychotic drugs prescribed to autistic patients were worthless, and in many cases caused more harm than good. Many autistic people developed facial tics because of ingesting such drugs, so David knew to keep Jared away from them. He was ahead of his time in many ways.

"But as crucial as his medical knowledge was, David was also very impatient with Jared, and I think frustrated with his condition in general. It always seemed to me that he viewed our son's disease as a constant thorn in his side, as if it was his fault, his cross to bear alone. I had to plead with David all the time to be kinder to his son."

This correlated with my theory that David had perhaps had a hand in ending his son's life. Granted, it was a long leap from being frustrated with your son all the time to slipping him a small pill and ending his life, but David had asked me to perform that very act on his sick wife. Was it such a stretch to believe he could have done the same thing to his autistic kid if he felt he could get away with it?

"Autistic children are not monsters, Alex, and I don't mean to imply that David and Jared were enemies as Jared grew up. There were many happy times, and in some ways, no one could make Jared laugh like David could. I think back on the time I spent raising my son, and it was the happiest period of my life."

Phyllis had a faraway look in her eyes. I reached out and touched her hand. "I know they're not monsters. It sounds like you had a good life with your son."

Tears pooled in her eyes, and I took my hand away from hers. "I'm sorry. I didn't mean to make you cry."

"No, no, it's okay." She was wiping her eyes. I looked on the counter for Kleenexes but didn't see any.

"Jared was a headstrong infant, more so than what you might see in a typical little boy. Early on, I would see these flashes of selfishness, this total inability to focus on or listen to what I was saying, and I just thought it was the normal behavior of a toddler. But there were other things, too. His loud voice, you see, that was always monotone; inabilities to retain or understand simple instructions or learning material.

"Later on, I discovered that Jared actually had remarkable talents and an ability to perform complex tasks that I wouldn't dream of knowing how to do myself, but it took a while for me to make those discoveries. Sometimes, in the beginning, all you can see are the limitations. At least that's how it was for *me* as a mother. But I got past all these things much faster than David. Jared's disabilities weighed heavier on David than they did on me. Even when he was improving and evolving as an adolescent, a teenager, and into adulthood, David oftentimes *still* couldn't get past the ... oh, I don't know, what he saw as the lack of maturity, the eccentricities, if you will, that poor Jared had as a five-year-old kid. It was like he was stuck in time, my husband. And to this day, I have to reprimand myself for not totally forgiving David for being that way. For almost looking down on the son that he also tried so hard to cure over the years. Sometimes I think David felt guilty about his behavior toward Jared, and that's why he spent so much of his life away from him, away from both of us, trying to find a cure for him, trying to make him better so that he would feel better about himself, better about our little family."

This was a lot for her to admit and for me to digest. All I

could say was, “It sounds like you were quite a mom, Phyllis. I can tell you did the best you could.”

“I suppose so, yes. I did at least do my best when it came to Jared.”

I smiled at her and looked at my watch. “Well, listen, I’ve taken up so much of your time. I should go.”

“I’m sorry for rambling. It’s just been so nice talking to you, talking to someone who’s actually interested. I get so lonely out in my big old house. And this job—it’s nice they took on an old lady part time, but it can go so slow. Look around—nobody else is even here.”

I shivered for some reason. “You have a real gift, Phyllis. Keep drawing.”

“I appreciate that. You can keep this drawing. I’ve got hundreds more at home,” she said, sliding the construction paper toward me. “Oh, wait.” Phyllis took the drawing back and said, “I add a Bible verse to all of them. What verse would you like me to write on this one?”

“Umm, I don’t know any Bible verses.”

“Here, I’ve got one,” Phyllis announced, leaning down to write. Her intensity writing the small, blocky words contrasted with her breezy way of sketching. When she was done, Phyllis held out the drawing for me to view, as if she were seeking finalized approval. The carefully formed passage was imprinted in the center of the hill. It read:

CREATE IN ME A CLEAN HEART, O GOD; AND RENEW A RIGHT SPIRIT WITHIN ME (Psalm 51:10).

“Very nice. I wouldn’t have thought of those words to add to such a pleasant picture, but I guess they’re meaningful. No offense,” I added with a nervous laugh.

“They’re words from David, the king of Israel, who killed a man’s wife and then murdered the husband, too, to try to cover up his first murder.”

“Oh.”

“I believe a truly penitent heart will receive the forgiveness of God, no matter what the evilness of the sins,” Phyllis informed me, "and that's what I like so much about David's words on such a seemingly 'pleasant picture,' as you so generously called it. I thought of another similar verse from Acts 3:19, but I like this one better."

"I'm just a little surprised. What could you possibly have to repent? Does this have something to do with ... you?"

She pondered my question. "The inability to forgive others myself sometimes, and the stagnating sin of harboring suspicions that keep me from always enjoying this true gift of life we all have, those are things I'm sinful of, yes. But we all, or most of us, anyway, take things for granted." She was smiling as she said all this, motioning in a heavy-handed way with her arm as if other people were around to take in her words.

"Well, thank you for sharing so much, and thank you for the drawing, Phyllis. It was really nice to meet you."

"You're most welcome."

As I walked out of the store, the words of David remained in my head.

And it wasn't the former king of Israel's proclamation of reconciliation that moved me so much.

Rather, I remembered what David Kendrick had mentioned at the cemetery, words that had popped into my head occasionally throughout the years and were uttered inside the warmth of my car as he and I and Trevor and Chad were attempting to bond.

David had told us how his wife reviled him with an intensity that was downright scary.

Chapter 17

On the day of the winter solstice, not long before Christmas, I quit my job and began doing part-time freelance work via a new online platform, mostly for clients who needed editing and copywriting jobs done. I'd just purchased a luxurious three-bedroom condo on the southwest side of town—for what I felt was a good deal at two hundred seventy-five thousand dollars—and figured I could work out of my beautiful second-floor office that offered a lake for a view.

To my chagrin, my workmates didn't have a going-away party for me at Hobby Town, where I'd worked for more than ten years. Feeling slighted, I brought up the issue with my supervisor, Debbie, during my last hour of work on my final day.

"What did you want us to do, Alex?" she asked, an unapologetic look on her face.

"Well, I guess what you do for everyone else who leaves. A little party with snacks and some cake, maybe lunch somewhere. *Anything* would have been nice."

Debbie took off her reading glasses while continuing to stare at me. "The truth is, and I think you know this, you've been *not* working here almost as much as you've been here these past several months. You've been checked out for some time now, Alex. I mean, you *do* realize that, right? It was getting to be a problem. We've talked about it several times."

"So no gathering together, no card, no cake—nothing at all? I've put in some good years here, done a lot for the company."

Debbie sighed. "Yes, you have. And I'm not unsympathetic with what you went through with your brother a few years ago—that was awful. But, just being really honest here, your days were numbered anyway. All the work you've been missing because of your vacation time and absences has really caused problems. You haven't kept up with your job duties, and what's worse is that you don't seem to *care* much about that fact. I'm sorry to be so blunt, but the general consensus around here is that you haven't been a very conscientious colleague."

I stalked out of her office without another word, glad to be done with the full-time working-world grind. At some point soon I'd start investing a sliver of my fortune and then have more money than I knew what to do with. Hell, maybe I'd start my own editing business or begin a novel. I had the chops to do those things.

Emily and I had started our divorce proceedings, a joyless, money-draining process that occurred in incremental steps. To her credit, she wasn't trying to pocket money from me, likely because she knew it was tainted.

I missed my wife a lot and kept wondering if she'd surprise me and give me a call, wanting to make up and reunite. My texts to her went unanswered except for one, which read: Please stop sending me texts. We're through.

I tried filling this emptiness by hitting the bars on my own a few times and even online dating, but these endeavors felt pointless. Life without Emily was hard to get used to, and I suspected it was going to affect me for years.

On the day before Christmas Eve, with the smell of takeout McDonald's burgers and fries in my car making my mouth water, I saw a man lying flat on his back on the sidewalk, right next to the large tree in my front yard. As I was staring at this unexpected sight on a gray, wintry day, I felt the car jolt. Confused, I pulled into my driveway, shut off the engine, and jumped out, leaving the McDonald's bag on the passenger-side seat.

I looked at the road and saw that I'd hit a black cat; that explained the bump I'd felt in the car. I raced toward the man, who was wearing gray sweatpants, a black sweatshirt, and a white headband. "Hey, are you okay?" I asked, leaning down and jiggling his tennis shoe. He appeared to be in his thirties and in great shape, not overweight at all. Then I looked closer at his face and saw it was a light shade of purple. I began CPR right away, remembering the process from my college days when I'd worked at a local swimming pool. After several minutes of doing chest compressions and breathing into his mouth, I saw that he'd regained his color. I pulled out my cell phone and dialed 9-1-1.

The paramedics arrived in minutes and took over. I stood back and admired their professional, speedy work. One woman from the paramedical team asked me a few questions. I told her what I'd seen and done as I was nearing my driveway, minus the info about the cat. Neighbors and passerby began to trickle in at the sight of the ambulance, asking me what had happened. Things became even more surreal when the owner of the cat I'd run over saw it on the road and began yelling and crying. That's when I decided to grab my lunch from the car, sneak into my condo, and watch the rest of the scene unfold from the front window. Not long after, the ambulance sped off.

It was Christmas day, and I was feeling joyful.

I'd purchased a beautiful fake tree that was dusted all over with some sort of powdery white substance that fell off in droves when the branches shook. But I didn't care: the tree made it seem like a genuine winter wonderland inside my condo.

Presents abounded underneath the tree, all shapes and sizes and with different kinds of festive wrapping paper. I loved the look and feel of the classic Christmas colors emanating from the floor and savored the creative designs of the wrapping paper. I remembered how I used to be so chintzy and would wrap presents for people using plain old newspaper. Emily had always chided me for that, and I realized now she had been right. Christmas deserved to be done in style.

It smelled like breakfast with a hint of sweetness in my condo.

Last night I'd put together a layered breakfast casserole, which was baking in the oven now. I'd risen at five this morning to make vanilla pudding, cookies, and cherry strudels. The desserts were now on the kitchen counter, and I'd tasted my share of them.

Walking into my family room with my plush blue bathrobe on, I said, "What present shall I open first? Ah, how about this one." Placing my coffee mug filled with hot chocolate on the coffee table, I kneeled down on the floor and scooted toward one of the larger presents under the tree. I ripped into it and was glad to see the large drawing of the "Farm in Wintertime" piece I'd purchased a few days ago in anticipation of today. I moved the picture aside, knowing exactly where I wanted to hang it later.

Sitting cross-legged by the tree, I opened all the presents. I'd gotten myself a backpack, dishware, a laptop computer, top-of-the-line headphones, a PlayStation 3, a small trampoline, new hardcover books, and some record albums for my new record player. Plus there was new furniture being delivered and an unassembled mountain bike in the garage. I planned on getting back in shape this spring.

Just because Emily was gone, I reasoned, didn't mean life had to be meaningless and boring. I had lots of money and to this point had been rather judicious with it, hadn't yet let loose with buying the new toys I felt I deserved after all I'd been through. That was going to change.

Kicking aside the mess of torn wrapping paper, I walked over to my stereo to turn up the volume. "Do They Know it's Christmas," my all-time favorite holiday tune, was playing, and I sang along with Bono. I slurped down the rest of my hot chocolate and went into the kitchen to pour some eggnog. Then I dug into the pudding, using the spoon that was already in the large bowl. Tomorrow I'd make bread pudding using my mom's classic recipe. I always added in more sugar than what the directions called for.

Back in the family room, I noticed an unopened present under the tree, so I opened it. "Oh, yeah," I said, smiling. I slipped on the rubbery old-man mask that had painted-on white hair on the sides, white eyebrows, and indented wrinkles on the cheeks. My smile stayed plastered on my face underneath the pungent thick rubber of the mask—I couldn't wait to see how I looked in the mirror. I stuck out my tongue through the mouth hole, wiggling it around.

Just then my oven beeped. I hopped to the kitchen and took the bubbling breakfast casserole out of the oven. It consisted of eggs, sausage, bacon, and cheese, all atop a layer of soft biscuits. I was stuffed already but couldn't wait to eat it. First it had to cool, though.

My cell phone buzzed in the pocket of my bathrobe. Frowning, I wondered who would interrupt a person's Christmas morning. Then I saw that it was my father and answered.

"What are you doing?" he asked.

"Celebrating Christmas, what do you think?"

"You sound muffled, Alex. Can you speak up?"

"Oh, sorry." I took off my mask. "I'm just enjoying my Christmas morning."

"Us too. Are you coming over later? Judy and I had planned on it."

"I am."

"Good." There was a pause and then Dad said, "Sounds like you've got the music cranked up over there. Do you have company?"

I laughed. "No. I turned up the stereo earlier and just haven't turned it back down. I'll bring your presents over today. I've got them in the car, wrapped and ready to go."

"Yeah, okay. That sounds good. Just bring yourself over here. That's what we want to see most, especially since we didn't see you on Thanksgiving."

"Yeah, I know. I'll be over later. Merry Christmas, Dad."

"Merry Christmas."

Chapter 18

One evening two months later, I was watching TV on the couch when the doorbell rang. I answered it and saw a youthful, attractive couple staring back at me. They were smiling, and the woman was holding a dish with tin foil over it. The man held a bouquet of flowers.

"Hi," the lady said. She had shoulder-length brown hair, a pretty smile, and a gleam in her eye that matched her ultra-white teeth. "We wanted to stop by and thank you personally for saving my husband's life."

"Oh, my gosh!" I exclaimed. "Please come in. It's so nice to finally meet you in person. I've heard a lot about both of you."

They stepped inside and the woman stuck out her hand. "I'm Marie, and this is my husband, Chris."

"Alex," I said, shaking her hand.

Chris and I exchanged a handshake and a half hug. "Really appreciate what you did," he said in a soft voice.

"Understatement of the year!" Marie exclaimed, and we all three laughed.

"Come on in. You can put the flowers and the food in the

kitchen," I told them, heading in that direction.

"I'd *love* to get a quick tour of the place if you wouldn't mind," Marie said. "It looks beautiful, and I've always wondered what these condos look like inside."

"She's a realtor," Chris informed me. "We live a few streets over on St. Peter."

So I gave Marie a ten-minute tour as Chris waited in the family room. He seemed more subdued than his wife, and he looked gaunt.

When we all three rejoined in the family room, I learned that Chris had had a one hundred percent blocked artery, which is what had crumpled him to the ground like a sack of potatoes during his jog.

"If you hadn't pulled into your driveway when you did, and given him CPR, the doctors said he could have had severe brain damage or even died," Marie said. "We can't thank you enough."

"Still have a long way to go until I'm fully recovered, but I'm feeling better every day," Chris said.

"I'll tell you what," I said to Chris, "if a guy like you can have a heart attack, I'm just wondering where that leaves the rest of us.

Look at me," I said, patting my formidable belly.

"Well, he has a history of heart disease in his family," Marie said. "He's got his orders from the doctor to abide by."

"Yeah, like what?" I asked, curious.

"You know, things like diet and medication and all that," Chris said. "I can't jog for a while, and I need to eat better." He talked with a slow drawl and was balding. I still couldn't believe someone as skinny and as young as him could have a heart attack.

"Speaking of food, we thought we couldn't go wrong with cherry cobbler," Marie said.

"Cherry cobbler?" I wasn't sure what she was talking about.

"Yeah, that's what we brought over for you. You'll have to try it and let us know how it tastes. I've never made it before."

"Oh, yeah, I'm sure it'll be great. Do you want to have some now?"

"No, better not," Chris answered. "*That's* the type of stuff I can't eat as much anymore, so she's been making it for other people."

"Well, just for other people who save my husband's life." We laughed and Marie said, "Yeah, we're trying to do the vegetarian thing. More fruits and vegetables, no meat, less sweets."

“Less fun,” Chris said.

“Do you live here alone?” Marie asked.

“Yeah, it’s just me. I’m going through a divorce. It’s almost finalized.”

“Oh, I’m sorry to hear that,” Marie said. I looked at Chris, who was staring at me in a sympathetic way. It seemed like I’d brought the happy mood down.

“Well, Marie already said it, but I truly can’t thank you enough. I mean, for you to be coming home when you did *and* to know CPR. It was just a real lucky thing.”

“A *blessed* thing is what it was,” Marie said.

I nodded, feeling a spark of pride. “You’re welcome. I’m so glad I was at the right place at the right time. It’ll do wonders for my afterlife karma, right?”

They laughed. “That’s right,” Chris said. “Cancel out all your bad deeds.”

“Oh, he’s a good guy,” Marie said. “I have a few single girlfriends. We should do a double-date night sometime.”

“Oh, well, yeah, maybe,” I said.

“Don’t sound so excited!” Marie joked.

“Sorry, Marie likes to do the matchmaker thing and sometimes gets overeager to set people up,” Chris said.

“Hey, I’m just putting it out there. I feel like we owe him.”

“I appreciate you looking out for me,” I told Marie. “It’s been rough and all, but I know I’ll eventually need to get out there again and date.”

“No rush on the dating front. Maybe I shouldn’t have mentioned that right now with you and your wife still going through a divorce. Here’s my card,” she said, handing it to me. “The three of us can go out sometime for dinner and a few drinks, with or without a fourth person.”

“That’d be great.” We stood up and I put my hand on Chris’s shoulder. “I hope you’re able to jog again soon.”

“Aw, that’s so sweet,” Marie said. She turned to Chris and gave him a sideways hug. “Life’s just so precious, you know?” Chris was smiling and looking down, putting his hands on her arm.

“Amen to that,” I said, feeling like I should say something.

They left and I shut the door, Marie’s words about life’s preciousness lingering in my head. I walked back to the couch and saw the imprints of where they'd been sitting just moments before. Sighing, I reached for the remote and started flipping through channels. I landed on a music station and saw a guy with curly blonde hair being interviewed. After a minute or two, I realized it was the guy from Def Leppard, the drummer who had lost his arm in a car crash. He was talking about the wreck he'd been in and how it had changed his life for the better, as well as how it had altered the band's course.

I shut off the TV and walked to the window, remembering the night Chad and Trevor had been talking about the one-armed drummer at my house while drinking, not long before they'd both met their end.

I looked outside. The lake had frozen over and you could see the gleams from backyard lights illuminating its surface. There were geese out there, stationed near the lake and huddled together. I wondered how the hell they could survive in such cold weather.

I started crying. At first the tears came out in short gasps, but then it became an all-out bawl.

I was a monster who had lied and killed for money, money just for me as it turned out. No amount of clean living was ever going to change that. My line to Chris and Marie about good karma during the afterlife had been stupid. The truth about my afterlife, if such a world existed, was that it most likely wasn't going to be pleasant. This thought kept me up at night, aged me.

Maybe that's why I didn't give a shit what I ate, and why I knew, deep down, I wouldn't be using my new bike to exercise all that much when the weather got warmer.

I just wanted to die so that I didn't have to remember what I'd done. If I suffered a heart attack like Chris, with luck it would snuff out my pathetic existence. Then I could get on with the afterlife punishment I deserved.

I wished the recurring dream—the one in which Trevor is hanging upside down like an overgrown bat from the top of the playground structure from which I'd toppled his friend to an early death, grinning at me with a sheet-white face in a foreboding manner—would go away.

Just the same I wished my *fond* memories of Trevor would go away as well. The story about his one-stand cross, his opening up about the Cyndi Lauper song, his revelation about coming out—it was all just as terrorizing to me as my horrific act at Cameron Park and what I'd done at the train tracks.

Because Trevor had chosen to love me, view me as someone he could talk to, and I'd chosen to not treasure those things. It was perhaps the worst of my sins.

All done for money, and nothing more.

Chapter 19

I wolfed down the third of my three Taco Bell bean burritos, no onions, not feeling guilty in the least. I'd lost thirty pounds since the night Chris and Marie had visited my condo, and had even gone out on a double date with them. I hadn't felt any sparks with the woman Marie had wanted me to meet, but that was okay. It had been a fun night.

I was officially divorced now, so life felt brand new. It helped that I was seeing a good therapist, someone who was easy to talk to and assisted me with getting out of the doldrums.

Today was the first day of spring and the weather was splendid, sunny and sixty-five degrees. Earlier I'd taken an eight-mile bike ride, my longest one yet, and now I was waiting in my kitchen for a reporter from the *C-U Journal* to come over. He was writing a story about Chris and wanted to talk to me for his piece.

The doorbell rang and I sprang up to get it, anxious to chat and contribute to the article. The reporter was a tall black guy, maybe six-foot-three or so, with closely cropped hair and an oval-shaped face with a goatee. I asked him to come in and offered him a drink.

"No, that's okay. I'm headed to Chris's house right after this since you guys live so close by. He took the day off of work. Figured I'd talk to you guys all in one afternoon."

"Yeah, that makes sense. Let's go out on the porch. It's such a nice day."

I lived on the second level and loved looking down at the lake. I'd never had a guest out on the balcony with me, so it was cool to be with someone whom I could share the view with. We saw right away, however, that it was too windy to talk outside. The reporter's gear was getting blown around, so we moved back inside. He sat on the couch, and I plopped down on a nearby chair. He asked me if it was okay to record our conversation, and I said yes.

"So what was going through your head when you saw Chris on the ground, man?" the reporter asked me.

"Hey, I'm sorry, but what is your name again? It's totally escaping me."

"Oh, sorry, did I not say? It's Richard. I've been at the *Journal* a few months now. Moved here with my wife from New York City. She's an adjunct instructor at the university."

"Nice. You like it here? Obviously it's way different than NYC."

"It is, yeah, but I do like it here. The slower pace kind of agrees with me." He smiled, and I could tell he wanted to get on with the interview.

"Okay, well, let's see. My thoughts when I saw Chris on the ground. I was just concerned, man, just really concerned."

Richard smiled and nodded. "All right, that's a good start. Why don't you take me through that day and afternoon. Tell me what you were doing before the incident. Tell me what the weather was like. Give me some details, as many as you can remember."

I rubbed my chin, thinking. This was going to be more difficult than I'd thought it would be. "Well, it was a while ago. It's hard to remember the particulars. Hey, what's your last name? Did you say?"

He regarded me for a moment and then said it was James.

"James," I repeated. "There's something familiar about you, but I guess I wouldn't know you if you just moved here."

"Yeah, probably not."

"Maybe I've seen your name in the paper. Well, anyway, let's see. It was a cold day, a typical winter day. I saw Chris on the ground and pulled into my driveway as fast as I could. I ran over to him and touched his shoe and asked him if he could hear me. Something like that. I didn't hear a response from him, and then I saw that his face was purple."

"What were you thinking at that point?"

"I didn't think. I gave him CPR, simple as that."

"Good." Richard was writing something in his notebook.

And then I remembered.

He was talking, asking a follow-up question, but I didn't hear him. He repeated his inquiry.

"I know who you are," I said. "I read about you in *Vanity Fair*."

Richard's face transformed. He went from the curious reporter to an exasperated transplant who hated being out in the Midwest sticks. He leaned back on the couch and we stared at one another. "Of course you did. A lot of people read that article and heard about it on TV. I understand if you want me to leave. It wouldn't be the first time."

"Oh, no. It's just so weird is all. Did you tell me your full name on the phone?"

"No, just my first name," he admitted.

"So people have been avoiding you because of what happened?"

He laughed. "Hell yes, they have. Either avoiding or berating. It was all I could do to get a writing job at the *C-U Journal*. I'm thankful for it, but it hasn't been easy, even here."

"Look, I ... I just want to say that nobody's perfect. I don't think what you did was all *that* bad. You didn't kill anyone or anything."

"Jesus, no. It wasn't that bad, but it was pretty bad. I'm just lucky to still be a journalist. I don't want to screw *this* gig up."

"So do you think you'll be at the *C-U Journal* long term, maybe try to make a go of it here?"

"If they'll have me." Richard shifted his position on the couch and said, "Listen, I'm not trying to be rude, but I do have to go see Chris after this. We should probably get on with the interview."

"If it makes you feel any better, I *did* kill someone. Actually two people. One person was my brother. And I got away with it."

Richard leaned forward. "What?"

"You heard me."

His eyes narrowed. "I can't tell if you're telling the truth or not."

"I am. I was with my brother and one of my brother's friends. My car broke down and we met a man who offered us five million dollars to kill his sick wife."

"Okay, go on."

"We took him up on it, and then later the old man had a heart attack right in front of me, right when he was giving me the cash, so I stole the money and left him there."

Richard shook his head. "You sure seem to run into your fair share of people having heart attacks."

"Yeah, I guess I do."

"You said the money was in cash?"

"Yep."

"So then what?"

"Well, it became this sort of fight among the three of us over how we were going to divide the money. At first we agreed to split it up three ways, but that changed. My brother and I decided we wanted to keep it just for the two of us, so we concocted a plan to eliminate the third guy."

"How'd you do that?"

"Well, I killed my brother's friend, at a park, and I tried—unsuccessfully, at first—to kill my brother. But I was able to kill him not long after."

"Why did you kill your own brother?"

"Take a wild guess, Richard."

He looked at me with a blank expression.

"I wanted the money all for myself."

"I see. How did you do it then? How did you kill them and get away with it?"

"God only knows how I got away with it. But I can tell you how I killed them. I pushed Chad off the top of a tall ledge at a playground and slit my brother's wrists on some deserted train tracks. Well, actually they weren't deserted. He ended up getting run over by a train, thus covering up the handiwork I did on his wrists."

"Holy shit! I *do* know about this. It was all over the news."

I couldn't help but smile. "Yep. Just like your story. We're alike, you and I."

I caught a look of distaste come across Richard's face.

"Jesus, dude. I can't believe you got away with all that."

"I know. I did talk to a cop once, right after it happened. My wife … well, my wife doesn't know about any of this. She's innocent."

"Good God. Why the hell are you telling me all this?"

"I don't know. I guess because we're kindred spirits. We've both done some stupid and bad things."

"I didn't kill anybody, man."

"True."

"Where's the money?"

"I've got it. It's safely tucked away."

Richard stood up and walked to the screen door that led to the porch. I had the sliding glass door open and a nice breeze coming in made the room feel pleasant. He stared outside for so long that I finally had to say something: "What are you thinking?" I asked.

He turned around. "That I'm not going to turn you in."

I smiled. "I didn't think you would. We're kindred spirits, after all."

"But I am going to have to take that money from you."

My smile vanished.

Now Richard grinned. "Yeah. Every single dollar bill that you have left."

"That's not going to work, Richard. I have a mortgage here. Look at this place."

“That’s too bad, pal. You killed two people. Figure out another way to pay your mortgage.”

“And if I don’t give you the money?”

“Real simple: I’ll turn your sorry ass in to the cops.”

“Like they’ll believe some dishonest, has-been journalist.”

“I’ve got your words on tape, you idiot.” Richard held up his tape recorder for me to see.

I tried my best to not appear crestfallen by this. “Did you record the part of the conversation where you tried to extort me, smart guy?”

“No, I pushed the stop button prior to getting to that part.”

“I guess you have it all figured out then, huh.”

He shrugged his shoulders. “Either way, life will be good for me. I either come off as a redemptive hero for capturing the *real* story about you, or I get to walk out of here a millionaire. For the record, I’d rather walk out of here a millionaire.”

I studied my clasped hands.

“What’s it going to be, sir? Your freedom from jail or your precious money?”

I looked up at him. “Why don’t you be the one to make up our ending? You're good at getting things wrong."

He waved his hand at me in a dismissive way. "I'll tell you once again the ending I prefer: go get the goddamned money, and make sure to bring all of it."

"I don't want to give you the money."

"Then you can go to jail. This isn't rocket science."

"How about I give you some of the money. Half."

"No deal. I want it all."

I sat still on the couch, thinking.

"I believe you told me your story because you have a guilty conscience," Richard said. "Once that money is no longer in your life, I think you'll feel better."

"Really? You think so?"

"I do. I really do."

"This isn't about me feeling better *without* the money. This is about you feeling better *with* the money."

He edged closer to where I was sitting. "Come on, man. It's time to give it up."

I shook my head in disgust. "Fine then, I'll give you the money.

But you better watch your back."

Richard laughed, but it sounded like a nervous laugh. "Fair enough. You watch what you do, too. Remember, it's all right here," he said, showing me the tape recorder again. "And, as you mentioned, I'm *good* at making things up. I could always spice up your little tale if needed."

"Sounds like you didn't learn much from your experience."

"Shut the hell up and go get that money."

I went to my bedroom, but I didn't get the money. When I came back out to the family room, I was holding a Smith & Wesson .357 magnum revolver I'd purchased three weeks ago. Richard saw it and gasped.

"Did you think of this ending?" I asked him, shooting him in the chest. He was moaning and squirming on the floor. Blood was coming out of his mouth, so I shot him again, waiting until he was still.

Then I turned the gun on myself.

The End

About the Author

Sal Nudo is the author of four books and has written numerous articles for various publications. He was the third-place recipient in 2015 of the Marian and Barney Brody Creative Feature Article Writing Award in Journalism from the College of Media at the University of Illinois at Urbana-Champaign. He earned a master's degree in journalism in 2016 from the same college. His novella, *The Newspaperman*, was selected as a Book Excellence Award Finalist by Literacy Excellence Incorporated and received the October 2018 Literary Titan Book Award (5 Gold Stars). He is a 2019 National Novel Writing Month winner.

Made in the USA
Middletown, DE
16 November 2022

15047847R00146